# Forgotten Retribution

Leigh Fields

Copyright © 2024 by Leigh Fields

All rights reserved.

No part of this publication may be reproduced, distributed, or transmitted in any form or by any means, including photocopying, recording, or other electronic or mechanical methods, without the prior written permission of the publisher, except as permitted by U.S. copyright law.

The story, all names, characters, and incidents portrayed in this production are fictitious. No identification with actual persons (living or deceased), places, buildings, and products is intended or should be inferred.

Book Cover by Getpremades.com

Not every story wraps itself up in a pretty bow. Sometimes things don't work out despite every sacrifice we make.

Not every story ends the way we want it to. Say the words before it's too late.

# contents

| | | |
|---|---|---|
| | Prologue | VII |
| 1. | Chapter 1 | 1 |
| 2. | Chapter 2 | 7 |
| 3. | Chapter 3 | 13 |
| 4. | Chapter 4 | 19 |
| 5. | Chapter 5 | 25 |
| 6. | Chapter 6 | 33 |
| 7. | Chapter 7 | 39 |
| 8. | Chapter 8 | 45 |
| 9. | Chapter 9 | 49 |
| 10. | Chapter 10 | 55 |
| 11. | Chapter 11 | 63 |
| 12. | Chapter 12 | 71 |
| 13. | Chapter 13 | 77 |

| 14. | Chapter 14 | 81 |
| 15. | Chapter 15 | 87 |
| 16. | Chapter 16 | 97 |
| 17. | Chapter 17 | 101 |
| 18. | Chapter 18 | 109 |
| 19. | Chapter 19 | 115 |
| 20. | Chapter 20 | 121 |
| 21. | Chapter 21 | 129 |
| 22. | Chapter 22 | 139 |
| 23. | Chapter 23 | 145 |
| 24. | Chapter 24 | 151 |
| 25. | Chapter 25 | 159 |
| 26. | Chapter 26 | 163 |
| 27. | Chapter 27 | 169 |
| 28. | Chapter 28 | 173 |
| 29. | Chapter 29 | 179 |
| 30. | Chapter 30 | 185 |
| 31. | Chapter 31 | 191 |
| Epilogue | | 195 |
| Afterword | | 199 |
| Of Dusk And Dawn Series | | 201 |
| About the author | | 203 |
| Also by Leigh | | 205 |
| Connect with me | | 207 |

# Prologue

## Lena

*Five months earlier…*

I stepped through the fog, and my sandaled feet sank into the sticky swamp mud.

My heart pounded in my ears. This is what it looked like outside of Atlantis.

I was never more thankful than in that moment for my flawed heritage. Orichalcum flowed through my veins, but not enough to keep me bound behind the cursed fog.

My feet carried me faster through the mud, and I clutched my toga in my hand to keep from tripping on it.

*"As the gods command, you must decide if you will stay in this world or join the humans in theirs. This is the time of your choosing."*

Calix's words echoed through my mind. What would I choose?

The gods abandoned the humans just as they had abandoned us.

At least the humans weren't cursed.

Maybe I would find what I was looking for out here among my father's people.

Maybe I would find freedom from the rules and regulations of my world.

Maybe here, I could choose my own path and not the one that was laid out before me.

The trees of the swamp began to thin, and I saw it for the first time.

The sun.

It beat down on my face, and I laughed as its heat hit me through the thick air. I spread out my arms and spun around, soaking it all in.

This was the sun.

No wonder Icharus was so fascinated with it.

"What is an Atlantean doing in Florida?"

I turned, and my eyes widened. The man before me crossed his arms over his chest, but really, he was no man.

His wide white wings tucked in behind him. The golden orichalcum weaved its way around him, shielding and hiding the wings from sight.

"Eudaemon," I whispered.

He chuckled. "You must be one of the flawed if you're here."

I looked around and realized the danger I was in. There was no one around.

We were alone.

I tried to pull my orichalcum, but it was nearly impossible to find in the human world.

"You don't have to worry about me hurting you. I'm here on a different mission." The eudaemon looked me up and down.

"What's your name?"

"Helena...Florakis."

He gave a subtle bow. "You can call me Drew. Let's call you Lena, huh? That will be easier among humans."

"Lena works for me."

He started walking along the black stone that stretched out into the horizon.

"Come on, Lena. Let's go find you some real clothes so you can fit in."

I looked behind me. I could go back.

But why would I?

Here I had a chance.

Here I could choose my own path.

Here...I could decide my own destiny.

I picked up the skirt of my toga and followed the eudaemon into my future.

# Chapter 1

## Seth

She *left*.

She actually left.

I crushed the letter in my hand and shoved it into the pocket of my cargo pants.

She had no right to decide for me.

She had no right to disappear.

If she thought she could hide, she was wrong.

I picked up my Glock off the counter and stormed out of my home, slapping the screen door as I passed.

"Seth, where are you going? Where's Lena?"

It was easy to ignore Drew as I passed him. My best friend could take it.

"Seth?"

My memories of her became painted in red as my fury rose. I couldn't see straight. *The girl I love wouldn't—no, couldn't—do this to me.* I stopped and gripped the side of the car. *But she did.*

Where was I going? She wasn't at her apartment, and if that letter was any indication, she wasn't anywhere.

I slammed my palm against the door and screamed at the sky.

The gravel crunched as Drew walked up behind me. "Where is she, Seth?"

Through my clenched jaw, I was able to get one word out. "Gone."

Drew leaned against the edge of the car next to me, the Florida humidity dampening his brow. "She loves you. What's going on?"

I stood straight and ran my hand over my hair. "She went to get her things at her place, and we were supposed to meet back here. She never showed, so I went to her apartment. It's completely bare. Nothing's left. No furniture. It's like she…vanished."

Drew shifted his weight and faced me. "There's got to be an explanation—"

"No. No, I came back here. Hoping. Praying she would be here." I pulled the letter out of my pocket and shoved it in his chest. "She left. She took the ring too."

"The *ring*?"

I scoffed. "Yeah. The bitch convinced me that she loved me back. I had my mother's ring all ready to propose."

"Oh, that's wrong."

My muscles tensed with the need to do something. Anything. I pulled my gun and emptied the chamber into the tree across the drive. Every clap of the bullet leaving the barrel eased a bit of my anger.

"Christ, Seth. Warn a guy, would you?" He glared at my display. He never approved of my reckless nature. Drew turned his attention to the letter in his hand. He cleared his throat before reading it aloud. *"I wish it were different, Seth. It's best if you just forget about me. I loved everything about our time together and I'll cherish those moments forever. My heart will always be yours, but our time was short. It was a summer love. Nothing more. Don't come for me. I won't be waiting. –Lena"*

Drew crumpled the letter and threw it over his shoulder. "Forget about her, Seth. She's not worth it."

I reloaded the gun out of habit and tucked it in the waistband at my back. "I loved her. That...that doesn't happen to me."

"She just got under your skin. Let's go find some other girls to make you forget."

I shook my head. "I don't want to forget, Drew. She took my trust and stomped all over it. She took my mother's ring. I want her to pay. I need to find her. She doesn't get the last word."

Drew raised a brow. "You said her apartment was emptied out. Where is she?"

I walked around him and picked up the letter, uncrumpling and smoothing it against my car. "She said more than once in this letter that she isn't coming back. People hide in all sorts of places, but in this part of the world? I'd bet she is headed straight to the entrance of Atlantis. She always got weird when one of the locals mentioned it—like she couldn't get away from the conversation fast enough."

Drew scoffed. "Seth, no one who goes in there ever comes back, if it even is Atlantis. You know as well as I do that the locals have always called it that. We don't know what's inside the fog. The army is crawling all over that reservation. We won't even get close to the entrance. She couldn't have made it either."

"Is that a challenge?" I turned and faced him, putting my hand on his shoulder. "It sounds like a challenge."

"No, Seth. It's not a challenge. Please forget about Lena. Forget about the ring. What about the sawmill?"

I clenched my fist and banged it against the top of the car. "None of it matters, Drew. She left! She had no right. She made promises. It's…I deserve an explanation."

"What if she doesn't have one? She could just be a horrible person. She made you love her and then she left. And she stole your mother's ring. That's low. Leave it alone."

I glanced at my friend, my brother-in-arms. "We fought side by side overseas, and now you're afraid of a little recon?"

"I'm not afraid. I'm trying to keep you from losing your mind. From doing something insane, like trying to find the entrance to Atlantis."

"I don't need to find it. We know where it is."

"Yeah, and we know that no one comes back out. Ever. You don't even know if she's there."

"I know it. I can just feel it…like it's pulsing through my veins."

We stared at each other over the hood of the car, neither backing down.

I jerked the car door open and dropped in behind the steering wheel.

Drew hopped in the passenger seat. "You're crazy."

"You're along for the ride."

"One more question before we go."

"Shoot."

"What are you going to do when you find her?"

I started the engine and floored the gas, kicking gravel up behind us.

"When I find Lena, I'm going to get revenge."

# Chapter 2

# Seth

Hours of listening to Drew wouldn't change my mind. He reminded me that I owned my dad's sawmill and there was no one left to run it. He reminded me that I had only known her for five months. He reminded me of every single stupid thing I had ever done, but it didn't matter. A fire burned inside me and rushed through my veins. When I pulled up to the reserve, my body was practically vibrating in my seat. I reached for the door handle but Drew's hand slapped down on my arm before I could open it.

"Tell me. What happens when you go in and she isn't there? Have you thought about that?"

"She's there. I can feel it."

"This is insane! There are at least a dozen other places she could be." He raised his brow. "You got some sort of sixth sense shit you wanna talk about?"

"Look, Drew. I appreciate you having my back, but you have to understand nothing is going to stop me from going in there."

I pushed my door open and went to the trunk. Drew followed. He was annoying sometimes, but he was important. I strapped knives to my ankle before tossing my go bag over my shoulder.

The Florida heat made the air thick with humidity. I looked at the swamp around us, mentally plotting the best path to the fog. It would be thick, and something was inside, so all the reports said. They just didn't know what.

"You realize this is probably the most reckless thing you've done. That includes jumping on that bull in Spain."

"Jumping on the bull was nothing." I looked up from my work and grinned at him. "That was fun. This isn't about fun."

"What about the sawmill?"

I clapped him on the arm. "Keep it going for me, will you?"

His face dropped. "You can't be serious."

I walked away from my friend and slung the backpack across my shoulder. "Dead serious."

"It's your dad's. Your family business."

I shrugged. "You're family, Drew. Plus, I want to know who is running it when I come back."

He jogged in front of me. "Seth, please don't do this. If you go in there, you won't return."

"That's just a myth. If I want to come back, I will. Let me deal with Lena, and I'll be back before you know it."

"Did you actually read the reports or not?"

I stretched my neck and ignored Drew. It didn't matter what was written on those pages. Nothing ever stood in my way before. Why would I worry about the details of coming home now? I had a mission.

Find Lena.

Make her *pay*.

Nothing else mattered.

"Okay, dumbass, I *did* read it," Drew called as he followed me.

I kept walking along the path to the nature reserve leading to the fog.

Drew kept pace behind me, and I yelled over my shoulder. "Well, I know you have about five minutes before you are coming with me through the entrance."

"Damnit Seth! This is serious."

I paused my walk, pondering all the times Dad wanted me to stop and think rather than react. I could do it…once. For the old man. "What?" I glanced down at my watch. "You now have two minutes to change my mind."

He put his hands on my shoulders and lowered his head to meet me eye to eye. "What if she is in there? What are you going to do? Kill her? Stalk her?"

"I'll do whatever hurts her most."

Seth dropped his arms and crossed them over his chest. "She isn't worth it, man. Seriously."

"She was." The whispered words fell from my mouth before I realized what I had said. "But that's all over now. I want her to feel what I feel."

"Okay, so let's say, for argument's sake, you find her and make her pay or whatever. Then what? You're stuck in some mythical land with no way back to the real world? We have no idea what's on the other side of that fog. There is a land mass and heat signatures, some of them too hot for humans. There is no telling what's actually in there."

"I'll figure it out."

"See, you say that, but it's not a plan. You can't go in there with no plan."

"Drew, if I don't come out in two months, come get me. But I'll be back. I promise."

"Okay, now that's a plan. Half of one. But it's better than what you had a minute ago."

"Can I go now, *Mom?*"

He punched my shoulder and pulled me close to slap me on the back. "Go. Get your revenge. I'll come save your sorry ass in two months if you can't figure it out."

I pushed him back playfully and grinned, spreading my arms wide as I walked backwards. "I'm the best. I'll be back before you even come up with your end of the plan."

"You do that!" Drew called after me.

I turned and walked down the path of the reserve. My boots sank partway in the soggy soil, slowing me enough to second-guess myself. What if she wasn't there? What if she didn't want me anymore? I loved her. She wanted to be free, but Lena didn't get to break my heart without feeling that pain herself.

The fog came into view, and I stood staring at the gray mist. I stretched my hand out, and it felt wrong. Thicker than normal fog, like the water droplets were made of plush.

It was now or never. Drew and I had read the reports about this area during our time in the military. The locals called it Atlantis, and the name stuck. It was surrounded by a thick fog that couldn't be penetrated by satellite. It covered enough land mass to hold a large city. There was no estimate of how many people were living there.

The reports stated that every military drone and human soldier who entered lost all contact as soon as they crossed the fog barrier. The men and women were presumed dead.

But I knew there was something else.

And I knew she was in there.

Deep in my soul, I knew it.

Lena.

My Lena.

And I was going to find her.

When I did, she was going to pay.

# Chapter 3

## Lena

I made a mistake.

I should never have come back, but I didn't have a choice.

What a fucked-up little thrill my mother would get from this.

I didn't come back because of the human world.

I came back *for* a human.

But I couldn't let her or anyone else know that.

I swallowed down my pride and buried the memories of Seth down as deep as they could go and knocked on the white stone door. It swung open, and my friend's eyes widened.

"Helena? You came back?"

"I told you I would."

Kassia wrapped me in a tight hug, her ringlet curls brushing against my cheek. "I can't believe you came back," she whispered. "It's been months."

I bit my lip. "It's good to see you too, Kassia."

She pulled back and snatched my hands. "You can't walk around Atlantis in those clothes. Come on. You can borrow mine."

I followed her into her home as a flood of memories washed over me. My shorts and t-shirt would stand out in the worst way here. I would stand out even more than when I arrived on the pavement of Florida in a toga. "Where is Evander?"

"He is working with the council."

"He's an intellect now?"

"No. He mostly does scribe work."

Kassia brought me a gold and blue dress with thick cords of gleaming yellow thread delicately attached to the bodice. I touched the silk and remembered how extravagantly I had dressed, even as a flawed.

I lifted my eyes to meet hers. "Are you happy with him, Kassia?"

"Of course. Why would you ask?"

I took the dress and stripped off my t-shirt and shorts. "In the human world, they choose their partners themselves."

Kassia became very quiet and busied herself helping me get into the dress. "Helena Florakis. It is one thing to spend your choosing time in the human world. It is another thing completely to try to bring it here. You came back. You knew what you would be returning to. There is no coming back. There is no changing Atlantis."

She fastened the top of the dress, and I felt the weight of my decision threaten to crush me. I began to braid and twist my blond hair as was proper for Atlantis. I would miss letting it fall freely around my shoulders like I did when I lived in the human world. Kassia took over once my dress was fastened.

She didn't comment about how much easier my hair was than hers to manage since it lacked curls.

Memories wanted to rush to the front of my mind, but I couldn't do that now. I had spent my choosing time in the human world. I had the choice, as all flawed do, to go into the human world or to remain in Atlantis. No one who went to the human world came back. And who would?

Well...now someone one had.

"I know. I knew."

Kassia turned my shoulders. "Selfishly, I'm glad you're here. I was afraid I would never see you again. Have you seen Dimos yet?"

The center of my chest ached. *I should want to see him. Right?*

He was my betrothed after all.

"Not yet. I...came here first."

Kassia smoothed down the fabric of her dress. "That was probably for the best. You looked...awful. At least now you can be presentable when you see him. You were so fortunate to be matched to an intellect."

It wasn't Dimos's face that came to mind. I shoved aside the green eyes and the dark hair. I ignored the memory of every touch, wishing to erase *him* from my mind. Even in my mind it was impossible to say his name.

"Yes. It was...fortunate."

She looped her arm with mine. "Who do you want to see first to tell them of your return? Your mother or Dimos?"

I shivered at the thought of my mother's condescending glare, but my guilt made me a coward.

"My mother. She is closer anyway."

I let my friend lead me down the steps and onto the gold streets. I wouldn't have paid them any attention, except the streets were black in the human world. Our streets in Atlantis lit up from beneath with the electricity from the orichalcum—light magic reflecting each Atlantean's divine heritage from the gods. The closer our lineage was to the gods, the more orichalcum flowed in our veins. My human father diluted the orichalcum in my blood, making it harder to do much more than feel its presence.

We passed the figures of Athena and Apollo, and I studied their faces as we passed. There were no stone statues lining the streets in the human world. Humans seemed to have forgotten the gods completely.

Not that it was much different in Atlantis. I hadn't ever seen a god or goddess appear, although the stories from our education said they used to walk here with us.

With the Atlanteans.

I reminded myself that was not who I was.

Not yet.

After the wedding, I could be considered a member of our society. But not before.

I was still a flawed.

"Helena. Are you listening?"

Kassia snapped her fingers in front of my face.

"Oh…no. What did you say?"

"The council thinks that there is a way to reverse the fog."

*The fog?* "What? That's not possible."

"That's what Evander told me. They were working on a way to reconnect with the rest of our world, as we were before the curse."

"The human world is so...different Kassia. It's not like it was centuries ago. Besides, the gods made the impenetrable. It was the punishment of Atlantis for advancing too quickly and going too far. It keeps those with orichalcum inside for a reason. Humans...they aren't ready for our knowledge."

"Of course, but surely the human world is different now. The gods have not walked among us in centuries. The council believes that they have forgotten about us."

I scoffed. "Evander is wrong, Kassia. There is no way the council would be working on that." I waved my hand around at the homes with large gray and white columns along the golden road. "Why would they ever want to leave this place? It is a paradise. Trust me, they aren't missing anything among the humans."

*Other than love. Other than freedom. Other than the right to choose their destiny.*

A voice cut through the air, sending shivers across my skin. "So my flawed daughter has decided to return?"

I jumped at my mother's voice behind me and turned to face her on the street. I took in her subtle glowing skin and her thick honey curls. Her sharp nose and cheekbones made her disappointed expression hurt more.

"Helena Florakis, you decided to come back to Atlantis? I'm sure your betrothed is relieved."

I bowed to my mother. "I have returned, Mother. And it is by your intellect and blessing that I was able to receive such a prominent match. I would be a fool for leaving that behind." I swallowed down the regret that rose up at my words.

"My blood deserves the best."

Rising to my full height, I stiffened my back and met her eyes. "I am grateful."

"Hmm. You were gone for so long, I believed you had chosen to stay with the humans. In fact, your choosing to go into the human world at all led me to believe you did not wish to be part of our society. Did you intend to stay and become frightened?"

Despite the turmoil of emotions swirling inside me, I kept myself poised. "No. There was no choice. Forgive me for my delay."

"It was quite a delay. Kassia, I will escort my daughter to her beloved. Thank you for bringing her to me."

My friend nodded and gave my hand a quick squeeze before leaving me to face my mother in the streets of Atlantis. Her choice for my union had surprised me when she told me before the choosing period. It seemed to be far above my station. Quite the unusual match for a flawed. She must have made many deals and used her position as leader of the council to arrange it.

Mother walked past me, and I turned to follow her as was expected.

"We will need to make the ceremony arrangements for you soon. I kept your housing intact, so your belongings should be there."

"Thank you, Mother."

We continued in silence, my heart numb.

As I squeezed the ring in my pocket, I knew it was a mistake to come back. Regret threatened to stop my heart and end my life right there in the streets of Atlantis.

How could I be so foolish?

# Chapter 4

# Lena

Every step down the road was heavy and exhausting. I wanted to sleep for maybe a decade or two.

"I will have to look at the council's schedule, but I believe we can make the arrangements for your union in a few weeks."

I jogged a few steps to catch up to my mother, her words bringing me back from my dismal thoughts.

"So soon?"

She stopped and turned her head to look at me. "Will that be a problem?

"No." I began walking again, hoping that my mother would drop what she would perceive as a slight. As the leader of our council, she was due the respect that came with her position, even from her daughter—especially from her daughter. "No. The sooner the union with Dimos is complete, the better."

But my mind lingered on Seth.

*Get him out of your head, Lena. You made a choice. Deal with it. No matter how shitty it is.*

"Will Dimos be at home?" I asked to shift the subject.

"Your betrothed is not with the council. It is not in session."

We turned down a lit, golden street and approached the steps up to Dimos's home.

*Please don't be home. Please don't be home.*

My mother knocked on the door, and I sucked in a breath as the human opened the door.

A lesser.

The lesser was marked—as all of them were—with three lines, one above the other, on her forearm. The young woman's only misfortune was having been born in Atlantis. She didn't even know that there was a whole world on the other side of the fog where humans were free.

I shoved aside my disgust. It wasn't like this in every part of the world. I knew that now.

Well, I knew that before I left. The difference was that now, I knew something could be done about it.

Becoming a lesser would be my fate if I were to break the law as a flawed. I stood on shaky ground from the moment of my birth. Would I rise in our society? Would the orichalcum in my blood be enough to keep me here? Or would I crash to the underside of our world? Would I be marked and forced into servitude as a lesser despite having one Atlantean parent?

"Is Master Dimos here?"

The lesser kept her eyes trained on the ground as she spoke. "He is."

"Will you let him know that Daphne and Helena Florakis are here to greet him."

I watched the lesser dip her head lower, never making eye contact, and turn as she shut the door.

"Are you relieved that you will be able to see your betrothed?" My mother's words were laced with...something. Relief? Warning? It certainly couldn't be concern or fear. She was not capable of those qualities.

I swallowed. I wasn't...I wasn't ready. Seeing Dimos would break my heart a million times over. It wasn't his eyes that drew me in. It wasn't his love I wanted.

But I lied...again. "Yes, of course, Mother."

She looked me up and down as if she didn't believe me. "I am glad you have returned."

I gave a polite smile. "I am as well."

The door opened again, and Dimos stood with his bronze-colored eyes scanning me. His voice shook as he said my name. "Helena."

I dipped my head. "Master Dimos."

He passed my mother and wrapped his arms around me, pulling me closer than was socially acceptable. "Helena. I didn't think you were coming back."

"I'm here." I squeezed my eyes shut tight to keep the tears from falling. *Wicked heart, stay locked in my chest. You cannot spill out now.*

I tilted my head back to look at him, and he laid his mouth on mine. I startled at the unceremonious display in front of my mother. It's not that we hadn't kissed before. It was...unexpected.

And...did nothing to stir my soul.

I slid my hand to his shoulder and pulled back. "Dimos."

My mother waved her hand and entered his home. "Don't worry, Helena. I have no problem with this display. You will be wed soon."

Dimos kissed my lips again and put his hands on my face. "Helena...you were gone for so long."

I stared into his bronze-colored eyes and wished I had never left. Now that I knew love, it would forever elude me here with him. My heart belonged to another. "Forgive me. I was...delayed."

He took my hand and guided me into his home. *Dimos must be doing well as an intellect.* His home was filled with golden statues and art on every wall, but I noticed the lessers more. They lined the walls, standing perfectly still with their heads tilted to the ground, awaiting their orders.

Humans born in our world, or the ones that came here by unfortunate circumstance, found themselves locked into this caste.

And those of us who were unlucky enough to be flawed? We would either be forced into servitude or binding ourselves to a member of a higher class. Either choice was a prison. I would have done better had I stayed outside the fog.

But I had to do something. Memories of Atlantis haunted me in the human world, forcing my hand.

Dimos touched my cheek. "I'm so glad you're back. I can't wait to wed you." He turned his attention to my mother. "Daphne, how soon can we make the arrangements?"

"She only just arrived. I was going to go to the council and book the ceremony after this stop."

"Good, good. A new session begins tomorrow. So probably a couple of weeks. Make it as soon as possible though."

Dimos pulled me into his lap as he sat on the stiff couch, and my mother sat in the seating across the room from us.

My eyes darted from her back to my betrothed, yet she seemed to pay his antics no mind. Physical displays were common but usually reserved for those who were wed. He took my face in his hands and brought my lips down to his. I draped my arms across his shoulders and resigned myself to this fate for as long as it lasted.

*Better get used to this.* This was the life I chose.

Dimos groaned and peppered kisses along my neck. "You taste of ambrosia," he murmured against my skin. "I prayed to the gods every day that you would come back."

"It was only a few months, Dimos."

"It was five months. Far too long to keep me waiting. I knew once our match was arranged that you were perfect for me."

He lifted his head and studied my face, the moments passing like a cruel eternity.

I gave him the smile he was looking for and put my hand on his cheek to satisfy his need. "I'm here now."

His length pressed into my thigh, and I shoved away the thoughts of having sex with him. He wasn't unattractive, but my heart could not be his. It belonged to someone I couldn't have, not if I wanted to live a life free of guilt.

*Forget Seth. It's over.*

"Come now, Helena. Let's get you back to your home. I need to go to the Acropolis before the scribes leave for the day."

I forced myself not to rise too quickly and give away my truth. Dimos put his hand on my lower back and guided us back outside his home. He roped me into his arms and kissed me like he would never see me again as we stood on the steps. When he finally pulled back, he kissed my forehead.

"I'll be counting down the days until we are wed."

"Me too," I whispered, hoping the remorse didn't come through my words.

"Come, Helena."

My plan would have to wait. I still had a part to play.

# CHAPTER 5

# Lena

"This is where we part ways, daughter. Can you find your path home from here?"

I glanced up and down the golden streets. "It hasn't been that long, Mother. I remember."

She studied me for a second before resting her hand on my shoulder, the gesture causing me to flinch. Affection was not her forte. Her eyes narrowed, and then she dropped her hand back to her side.

"I am...grateful you made a wise choice, Helena."

"Thank you, Mother."

She clasped her hands before herself and turned to go to the acropolis.

I waited until she left to dart the opposite way from my home. There was one other person I had to see—the one who haunted my mind in the human world.

It was hard to keep my steps even and not draw attention to myself. When I was sure no one was looking, I dashed down the alley beside the large stone home hoping to avoid everyone, including Calix. At the end of the alley, I knocked on the small wooden door.

I chewed on my lip and angled myself away from the street.

Not that it would help. If anyone noticed me here, it would be unusual. My clothes alone would tell them I shouldn't be in such an alley, where the lessers traveled.

The door opened, and his dark eyes found mine.

"Helena."

He wrapped his hand around my arm and pulled me into the small quarters, shutting the door behind us.

"You shouldn't have returned, Helena!"

I choked back the tears at the way his voice broke. "I don't think my heart would let me make any other choice, Dad. I'm going to find a way to free you from this place."

He tightened his grip on me, and I buried my face in his chest. The rough wool of his tunic scratched my face, but it didn't matter. I went months without seeing him and I'd endure worse to see him in better circumstances.

"You had a chance, Helena. I made the mistake of stumbling through the fog all those years ago. The council gave you an opportunity to go to the human world. We talked about this. You should have taken it."

I shook my head. "I can help."

He pushed me away from him. "You have to leave, now. Before anyone knows you are here. You can make it back. You're human enough."

"It's too late for that, Dad. I saw Mother and Dimos already."

His face paled. "Gods above. You are too selfless for your own good, Helena."

The tears spilled down my face. "No. This is wrong. I know that even more now. Did you know humans don't enslave each other outside the fog? They're free! Dad, it doesn't have to be this way."

He gripped my shoulders, and his fingers dug into my skin. "Helena. Forget about that. Forget about any of it. You're not there anymore. You'll end up a lesser or worse if you keep talking like that."

I shook my head. "No, Dad. I'm going to free you. All of you. Our city...it's not right."

He put his hands on my face, and the brand of three lines, one above the other, on his forearm brought bile to my throat. He stroked his thumbs across my cheek, as his whispered words broke my heart. "You are far more important to me than my freedom. You have to leave. Please, Helena. Promise me that you will not stay."

I met his eyes, worn with years of fatigue and work. "I...I don't think I can do that."

He dropped his hands. "Then, please, for the love of your father, marry that boy and forget about this foolish idea of freedom for me. I knew love and happiness, even if it did not last. All I want for my precious daughter is a life filled with joy. And safety."

Fresh tears spilled fresh over my cheeks again. Happiness was far away on the other side of Florida with a man who would never forgive me, even if I did return.

"Okay, Dad. I'll do it."

He pulled me into his chest, and I clung to him, wishing the moment would last.

"Precious Helena, I only want what is best for you. One day, a light unfolds in the darkness, beginning what will have no end, so the gods say. And I want that light for you. A light of happiness and joy."

He kissed my temple and released me.

"Leave now, Helena. I don't want to see you here again. Go and live your life with all happiness. Never return."

I couldn't look at him as I left. He was right. I shouldn't have been there at all. A flawed who mingled with a lesser was asking for enforcers to come and send her to the trials. These stolen moments would have to be the last until I could free him. *Them. All of them.*

So I let the tears leave trails down my face and neck as I fled out of the lesser quarters and through the alley. I pulled the skirt of my dress up and ran. I didn't care that I was supposed to be blending in. I wanted to be free, even if it was only for a moment, so I ran. I raced the last several blocks to my home and up the steps, slamming the door closed behind myself and collapsing in the foyer on my knees.

How did I make so many mistakes back to back in such a short time? *Shouldn't there be a limit on the idiocy one person could commit in a week?*

Like Sisyphus pushing the stone up the hill, I made more and more work for myself without any results.

All at the expense of my heart.

*Thirty- six hours earlier...*

I glanced around the cluttered office. *How long had Seth left this stuff here?* His dad died a few years ago, and it looked like he hadn't been in here after that day. It was the least I could do for him since...

Since I needed to leave to free my own dad and the other lessers.

The files were full of dust, and I sneezed as one slipped from my hand. I didn't have time for this. I sniffed and held the tears back. Seth wanted to pick me up at my place in an hour, and I needed to be gone. Long gone.

I couldn't help myself though. I wanted to do something for him. Even if it was just this small act of cleaning up his dad's long-abandoned office.

The photos scattered on the floor. I wouldn't have paid any attention, but we were in the sawmill office, and these photos were…romantic. I picked up the one closest to me.

The man was obviously Seth's dad, Graham. I had seen his picture in Seth's house.

But the woman?

Seth said that his mother had died long ago.

My hands shook as I lifted the picture closer.

His mother was certainly not dead.

I would know that face anywhere. We learned about her in our education. She had blocked the prayers of humans to the gods. She left chaos and misery in her wake. Her depiction was surrounded by words of warning in our primary books.

I bit my lip. I had to run. I had to go.

Seth's past was his business. I had my own parental drama to sort out, but now I knew how much danger he was in if he were to find his way to Atlantis.

I hadn't planned on doing anything. I was going to simply disappear.

Now?

Now, I knew I had to break his heart. He couldn't follow me back there. He would be able to follow me if he wanted to. And if he did…

"What are you doing in here?" My head whipped up to the doorway. Drew stood there, staring at the photos on the floor.

"I…"

"You don't have much time. I thought you were going back to Atlantis."

"I was—I am. You can't let him follow me." I held up the photo, my hand still shaking with the knowledge of Seth's heritage. "Especially…"

"I know. I have my job. You have yours." Drew crossed his arms over his chest.

"If he goes there…he can't leave." I scrambled to put the files back in the cabinet.

"You worry about getting back. I'll worry about Seth. He's my responsibility."

"Drew, he can't—"

The eudaemon let his wings out and spread them wide as his eyes glowed with orichalcum. "Get out of here, Lena. I have no interest in arguing with your kind. You would think that a flawed would see the choosing time for what it was. A gift. It's your only chance to live for you and you're throwing it away." Drew tucked his wings back behind him and made them invisible once again before muttering, "He had to fall for an Atlantean."

I shoved the cabinet door closed. "I know…I…"

"I get it. Trust me. I do. You have to go. Gods only know what is happening in Atlantis these days…" Drew ran his hand over his short hair. "But he's going to lose it. I doubt his heart will ever recover from this. And now you're out of time."

I stepped around the eudaemon with caution. He had his work cut out for him, and I didn't envy his job. Recklessness and impulsivity were as easy to Seth as breathing.

I rushed out to the car and checked the time.

Seth would have left his home by now.

A letter. That's how I would make sure that he wouldn't come after me. Make it clear I didn't just disappear; make him understand that I left.

I raced the car to Seth's property and spun in the gravel of his drive as I arrived. I threw open the screen door and paused to freeze the memory of this place in my mind.

*Keep moving, Lena.* My heart pounded as if trying to escape my chest as I ran up the stairs to his room. I stopped dead in the doorway. On the bed was a box, small and blue.

No...

It would hurt, but I had to see it.

I had to know...

Was his love for me as deep as mine for him?

The blue box popped open with the slightest pressure from my fingers. The gold was lined with orichalcum, that much was clear. I traced the lightning symbol on the side and the red garnet stone. This ring...

It was Aite's. It had her symbol.

He did love me. Enough to give me his mother's ring.

Tears streamed down my face. I shoved the ring in my pocket. I shouldn't have, but it would help keep him safe. If he did ever make it to Atlantis, it would be everything he needed to save him from the council. But if I could keep it hidden—keep him hidden—that was for the best. No one could know.

I ripped a page from one of his journals to write my letter. His words jumped off the lines, begging to be read.

"'Lena is moving in today. It's going to be a great day.'"

I slammed it closed and kissed the leather.

I wanted that too. A future here with Seth. So much.

And the worst part was…he would never know.

I penned the words I knew would hurt him, but they would keep him far away from me.

"'I wish it were different, Seth. It's best if you just forget about me. I loved everything about our time together and I'll cherish those moments forever. My heart will always be yours, but our time was short. It was a summer love. Nothing more. Don't come for me. I won't be waiting. —Lena'"

I swiped away the tears and laid it on the bed so he was sure to see it.

Time to go.

Back to where the fates pulled on my strings. Back to where my choices were stolen from me. Back to where I would never know love again.

But this way I could save my father.

When the memory ended, I lifted my head to look at my home. The reminder of my choices settling in my mind with regret.

I should have prayed Seth would forgive me.

But I knew better than to hope.

Hope died in Atlantis a long time ago.

# Chapter 6

## Seth

The fog vibrated and hummed against my skin. Something was different about this fog, that much was clear. I held the gun in front of me, wondering how far until I reached the other side.

Was there another side?

By my best estimation, I was about a hundred yards into the fog when it began to shimmer and lessen. Light reflected on the beads of moisture. Where was the sun? There couldn't be any sun here.

One more step, and the answers were clear. A city in the distance was lit with electricity and covered in gold, which caused the light to reflect into the fog, creating their own version of sunlight. What was this place?

There was nothing to shield me from being seen. The sand was out of place beneath my feet. Even the air felt different, like this place was picked up from across the world and dropped in the Florida swamp.

I chuckled to myself. If the legends were true and this was actually Atlantis…that's exactly what the gods did.

What complete bullshit.

There was no wall or barrier around the city. No means of defense. It put me on edge.

What city didn't have a boundary?

I holstered my gun and moved toward the rising structures. The homes were all made of stone, the smaller ones on the outside and the taller ones toward the center of the city. There were no people outside the perimeter. No guards that I could see. No sentries watching for intruders.

It was easy to slip between the stone walls of the buildings and walk along the lit golden streets. Streets of gold? It was absurd.

I positioned myself along an alley and watched the people that resided there. A woman in a drab gray dress carried an overflowing basket of items. She had a tattoo on her forearm of three lines, one right over the other.

"Excuse me." I stepped in front of her.

Her eyes widened, and she dropped the basket in her hand. I knelt to help her collect the items.

"You…you shouldn't be here." She snatched the cloth from my hand. "Leave. Leave now."

"I was hoping you could help me."

She shook her head violently. "Leave. That is your only hope. You can't be here."

"I'm looking for someone."

"Whoever you are looking for is dead or worse. Go!" She actually reached out and pushed my arm.

I rose to my full height.

"Look, lady. I don't know what you think is going on, but I'm looking for a woman. She came in here and—"

"If she came in here, she is lost. Your only hope is to leave."

The woman rushed to gather her things and scurried past me down the street. I watched her retreat down another alley further into the city.

I followed the path she took and continued to watch for soldiers or law enforcement of some kind. They were always easy to spot. Armed with some form of weaponry. Constantly scanning their surroundings. Still, there were none.

The alleys were easy to navigate, and the streets became wider the further into the city I went. The appearance of people became more frequent, and I studied their behavior from the shadows.

Their clothes were odd, like I had stepped back in time. They seemed…Roman? Mediterranean? The structures had many columns, and some of them had marble steps. There did not seem to be a lack of wealth here.

But there did seem to be a class difference. Some of the people looked like the first woman, dressed in drab gray clothing. The others had flowing dresses and ornate tunics. I slid along the wall and looked around the corner.

*There*…I knew there would be some form of soldier here.

The man stood with a sword on his hip and a black, sleeveless top that showed his strength. He didn't appear to be guarding anything in particular.

Likely just a guard on patrol.

I followed the alley back away from the guard, turning further into the city.

Where would I find Lena?

She could hide, but not forever.

A flash of blonde hair and a figure I would always know grabbed my attention. I melted back into the shadows and watched.

I had found her. That was easier than it should have been.

My first reaction was relief. I wasn't crazy. She *had* come through the fog. I did know her. I knew she came through the fog. I don't know how, but I knew it.

Relief quickly faded away into rage.

She stood on the steps with an older woman, but I hardly noticed her. The man with his arms wrapped around Lena had my full attention.

*How dare he put his hands on her!*

I clenched my fist, and my heart began to pound when he laid his lips to hers like a lost lover.

She didn't push him away.

She didn't try to leave.

No. That traitorous bitch leaned into him and smiled before walking down the steps with the woman.

If she thought she would get a happily ever after, she was wrong.

I trailed the two women. My fingers traced the edge of my glock, itching to release the tension in my body. Lena finally separated from the woman and backtracked past me. It was more difficult to follow her this time. She was trying to avoid attention and she was better at it than I anticipated. I saw her enter an alley, but it was a dead end.

*Where was she?*

I almost walked down the alley to the small door at the end, but she appeared back in the street, saving me the trouble. So I stalked her to what I assumed was her home.

Checking the streets and not seeing anyone watching, I marched up the steps and threw the door open before storming in.

Lena jumped and held her hands to her chest. Her eyes widened, and she stepped back away from me.

Good.

She should be afraid.

I kicked the door closed behind me.

"Hello, Lena. Miss me?"

# Chapter 7

# Lena

"Seth." *He can't be here. He can't be this stupid.* "You have to go."

I stepped toward him. He raised a gun and pointed it at my chest. My heart froze and then sped to a gallop. I raised my hands and backed away.

"Seth…"

"Lena."

He followed me with his gun raised.

Idiot. He wouldn't pull the trigger. He must know that.

I retreated until my back was against the wall and he stood with his raised weapon a few feet away. When he didn't move closer or make another move, I crossed my arms and raised a brow.

"Seth, pull the trigger if that's what you're here for."

"Don't try to talk me down, Lena." His words were laced with ice.

"Talk you down?" I scoffed. "I just told you to kill me." Pushing off the wall, I walked toward him and pressed my chest into the end of his gun. His face betrayed him with the slightest twitch of his lips. "You don't want to kill me. If you did, you would have already pulled the trigger. You would have pulled it the second you walked through the door."

He stood there taking in my words. *His body must be humming with all the orichalcum in this place.* Did he notice the difference? How the orichalcum in his veins responded to the magic thrumming in our streets? He probably didn't even understand why he was feeling the power.

"You're right. I don't want to kill you." He set the gun down on the table and closed the remaining distance between us.

I inhaled as his body pressed against mine. It hadn't even been two days, and I missed the way he smelled. I missed his touch. I missed the way he looked at me.

His hand snaked around the back of my neck, and he gripped my hair. He leaned close, and his lips tickled my ear as he spoke. "You're right. I don't want to kill you. I want to *ruin* you."

I shouldn't have been surprised. I should have pulled away. I should have kicked him between the legs. But when he angled my face towards him, I gripped his shoulders and pressed my lips to his, unable to resist.

What a reckless idiot I was.

Seth parted my lips, and his tongue tangled with mine, his fingers tightening in my hair. I lost myself in the way he unraveled my soul. How was a simple kiss my undoing?

He broke apart before I was ready to let him go, pushing back from me and leaving me leaning toward him…wanting more.

"You smell like him."

"Who?"

"The man you stood on the steps kissing an hour ago."

My breath locked in my chest. *He saw me. He saw me with Dimos.*

*Oh gods…*

"I can explain—"

"Don't bother, Lena." He turned around and waved his hand in the air.

Tears welled up in my eyes while I stared at his back. I loved this man in front of me. I still wanted him.

Did I make a mistake? Did I mess up by trying to save someone else?

Yes…

"I'm…sorry, Seth. I love you—"

He turned and cut off my words with his glare. "How dare you! How dare you say you're sorry! His kiss is still on your tongue. His smell is on your clothes, your skin."

He picked up the gun and put it in a holster.

My throat choked on the tears beginning to fall down my cheeks. My heart pounded faster at the realization of how much danger he was in. He shouldn't be here. "Seth, please…you have to listen—"

"Listen to what? To you say you love me? I'm not here for your pretty lies, Lena."

I stepped closer, but he held up his hand, keeping the space between us. "I'm so sorry. You shouldn't have chased me down."

"Don't put this on me."

"Seth, if we could have stayed frozen back home, I would have. I've been running from this ending since I fell for you."

"Is that how you sleep at night? Convincing yourself that you loved me?"

I threw my hands out beside me wide on either side. "Love is damage, Seth. Please, do us both a favor and kill me now."

Seth marched back into my space. I looked up at him and waited, letting my arms drift back down to my sides. His heavy breathing and tense shoulders reminded me that he was struggling. Good. He wouldn't find out the truth if he shut himself off.

Seth trailed his fingers along my cheek. "Such a pretty face. I did love you." His fingers gripped my chin.

I clenched my jaw. I wanted to tell him how deeply I cared for him. How I carried the secrets to keep those I loved safe. If he had any chance of surviving, he had to leave. If the council knew he was here…

"I take it back. I'm not sorry, Seth. I don't love you. You can't kill what has already died."

He smiled. "Lena, Lena, Lena. We're past lies now aren't we?"

I should never have left.

I should have never come back.

How did I try to do the right thing and end up hurting everyone around me?

I was locked into a life as Dimos's wife in a godsdamned city. My father was still a lesser. My mother still fulfilled her duties on the council.

The love of my life was in danger and he hated me too much to listen to me.

How in Hades's name was I going to get him out of here?

*Don't pray.*

*The gods can't help us here.*

# Chapter 8

# Seth

She looked so beautiful it made me sick.
How dare she try to apologize? Or even speak to me?
She didn't love me.
Maybe she did—
No. She didn't. She wouldn't have left.
"You knew what you meant to me. You even took the ring. You had no right."
Her face dropped. "If I give it back will you leave?"
She wanted me to leave?
*Too bad, Lena.*
"You're not going to get rid of me that easily. You lied to me. You stole what wasn't yours. You tricked me into loving you. You have to pay for that."
She put her hands on her hips and raised a brow. Who did she think she was? She didn't get to give me that look. I wasn't the one who fucked this up.

"You're such a child, Seth. What are you going to do? Follow me around and call me names? Grow up. Go back home. Where is Drew? I can't believe he let you come through the fog."

"Why do you care about Drew? Were you screwing him too?"

She crossed her arms over her chest and tilted her head to the left in the slightest way, a look that told me she was furious. Good. I wanted to see her affected.

"No. I haven't been *screwing* anyone."

"Just kissing men on the steps."

"One man. And last time I checked, I left you. I broke it off. That means I'm single, and I can kiss who I want."

Her words cut. I couldn't be thinking of her as mine. She wasn't mine. Not anymore.

Lena turned her back to me and went to the small kitchen. She pulled a glass down from the cabinet and filled it with water. She slid it across the stone counter toward me and took another one down for herself.

I took the water and watched her. She was dressed in a long flowing dress. It didn't show the curves I knew were underneath the fabric. I preferred her in the tight low-cut tops she wore back home.

Visions of her in the office of the sawmill flooded my mind.

I looked up from the office chair as the door opened. I wasn't expecting anyone. Dad had left the tax information in one of the file cabinets here, and I needed to see if we were making the same amount as before he died. It was infuriating. His records were everywhere.

Why didn't he ask me for help before he got sick?

"The guy at the front said to talk to you. I'm looking for a job."

The owner of the voice was a beautiful blonde with curves for days. I scanned her up and down before I found my words. "What?"

"The guy...Drew, I think. He told me to come back here and talk to you about a job."

"Oh...yes. I did put an ad in the paper."

"For an office manager. I know. That's why I'm here." She tilted her head to the left, ever so slightly. Was she nervous?

"Of course." I stood and extended my hand. "Seth."

She gripped my hand firmly. "Helena. But please call me Lena."

She had intrigued me when I first met her. Lena was direct and clear. She wanted a job and she intended to get it.

What happened?

That girl—the one who spoke clearly and told me what she wanted—where was she?

"Why did you do it, Lena?"

She glanced at me before running her finger over the rim of the glass. "It doesn't matter, does it?"

"It doesn't matter? You told me you loved me. Ha! If you really loved me, it would matter to you."

She sighed, and I knew that my words were working their way under her skin. "Seth...it's more complicated than that."

"Yeah. You've got another boyfriend."

She cleared her throat. "He's my fiancé, actually."

I didn't realize that words could slice through my chest and make it hard to breathe.

"Your...fiancé?"

"Yes. That's why I broke things off."

It took everything in me not to turn and leave the home. But that's exactly what she would want, and I wouldn't give her the satisfaction. I would wait and put a bullet between that man's eyes another time.

"What is it, Lena? Does he have money? You didn't strike me as a money whore. Maybe you like his manners or status? Go ahead and enjoy that."

I crossed the space between us, crowding her against the counter.

"You can go be lonely and unsatisfied every night knowing that there is someone out there who knows how to make you scream and moan. Someone who knows every inch of your body and wants nothing more than to enjoy it. Oh wait. Let me rephrase. *Wanted*…not wants."

Her eyes glistened with unshed tears. Lena was too stubborn to let them fall, but I knew my words struck true.

"You're a monster."

I leaned closer so that my lips could brush against her hair as I spoke. "You created this monster, Lena."

# Chapter 9

# Lena

I shoved his chest and pushed past him. "Get out of here, Seth. I don't want to see you anymore."

"Better get used to me, Lena. I'm going to be here to ruin every moment for you until I'm satisfied that you have felt as much pain as you've caused."

*That's it!* He was a complete and utter idiot. Where was Drew? This man was in real need of a eudaemon's protection now, if for no other reason than I would kill him myself.

I turned to say the words that would cut him deep, when light from the outside flooded into my home. I spun and saw the orichalcum that glowed from my mother's hand.

"Helena!"

I raised my hands and put myself between her and Seth, who had already drawn his gun and aimed it at her head. Not that it would matter. The orichalcum would stop any bullet.

"Mother, he is not what you think."

"Mother? This is your mom?" Seth's confusion was understandable. I told him my parents were gone. It wasn't a direct lie, but it wasn't the truth.

"If you brought a human here, you are more selfish than I imagined you to be, Helena." My mother's eyes darted between Seth and me. "You know what happens to humans here."

"What happens?" Seth growled.

I cut Mother off before she could answer Seth. "He is not what you think. You should let him go."

"I'm not going anywhere."

"He's not going anywhere…except to the council." My mother's stare hardened, and I knew there would be no turning back.

I looked between them before shaking my head and rubbing out the tension building in my neck. "You both are more foolish than Echo to tempt the gods this way. Go back to Florida, Seth. Mother, do not mention his existence to anyone. Especially not the council."

Seth put his gun away and stepped closer. He eyed me as he moved around to my mother. He extended his hand.

"Seth. I'm here to ruin your daughter."

My mother furrowed her brows, and the orichalcum faded as she took his hand in hers. "Daphne. Ruin her?"

"She took something that wasn't hers. She lied. I'm here to make sure she feels the same pain she caused."

"How very…hmm—may Themis bless your intentions."

I scoffed. Of course my mother would agree with Seth. She had no idea how dangerous he was here. The gods would see him destroyed, even if it meant returning to the desolation that was Atlantis to hunt him down themselves. How they had not discovered his existence before was astounding.

I took the ring out of my pocket and shoved it into Seth's chest. "Take it and leave, Seth. This is your last chance!" I squeezed my eyes shut and held back the tears, swallowing through the thickness in my throat. "P-please."

He took the ring and held it between his thumb and forefinger. His eyes darted from the ring back to my face. "Why would you take it only to give it back?"

"Gods above…" My mother stepped closer and grabbed Seth's wrist, examining the ring. "Is it true?"

"Mother…don't."

"Aite…She hasn't been seen…Does she still walk among the mortals?" Mother's eyes scanned over Seth's body. "Is that ring yours?"

"It was—"

"It's his." I cut off Seth's words. He looked at me and then back to my mother before nodding. I put my hand over my mother's. At least without direct confirmation, he wouldn't be sent to the helpers right away. The longer his identity remained a secret, the better for him.

My mother dropped his wrist and I let my hand fall to my side. "You should keep that close. Come. We need to go to the council."

I locked eyes with her. "I thought they were not in session, Mother."

"I think this calls for an emergency session. Aite has been walking among the humans. It could be a sign."

"Are the council your leaders?" Seth seemed to finally notice something other than his own feelings for a change.

My mother walked out the front door, and I went to follow her when Seth wrapped his hand around my arm.

"What?"

"Did you say they are the leaders? And is this really Atlantis? Lena, what is going on?"

"Where did you think we were? And did you think I would dress like this for fun?" I gestured to the long dress.

"Why are we going to the council?"

I stared at him for a moment. Did I dare to tell him what he clearly did not know and put him at risk?

I chewed on my lip while I considered my options. For once, Seth waited, and the silence dragged out between us.

"My mother believes that you are the child of one of our goddesses. She wants to take you to the council to decide how they should use you."

"That's insane…because my mother died."

I remained silent. Aite was far from dead, but the son of the goddess of mischief and ruin held far more power here than he realized. If he lost control…

Seth dropped my arm and the memory of his touch haunted me. He ran his hand over his short-cropped hair. "What happens with the council if my mother is who you say?"

I swallowed, the words sticking in my throat as I stared into his green eyes.

"Helena, are you coming?" My mother held the orichalcum light in her hand, ready to lead the way.

"Of course, Mother."

I looked back at Seth, and we began walking down the stone steps of my home. I leaned and whispered to him before we could close the distance to my mother.

"Do not ever confirm it. Keep the ring close. Don't let them know. And for the love of the gods, Seth, control your temper."

# Chapter 10

# Seth

"What does that mean?" I hissed at her.

"Shhh." Lena glared over her shoulder.

She had no business looking as sexy as she did in that toga thing. It was messing with my head.

Lena was the one that lied. Such pretty lies she told me though.

*She loved me.*

*I was the only one for her.*

I shook my head free of the memories and let my eyes scan our surroundings instead of her ass. The streets were lit from beneath. The gold gave off a low light in the nighttime. Was the level of the light on the streets how they had determined night and day?

The fog above us was still as thick and gray as it was before—an almost black veil between this world and mine. No stars shone down as they would have outside. *What direction were we even headed?*

The further into the city we went, street lamps lit the way. There were more men in black shirts. They were the guards or police in this place. Where were their weapons?

One of them lit their hand with the same golden glow Lena's mother had, and it hit me—the light was dangerous. Was it fire? Some sort of plasma?

I ran my hand over my hair and pressed my thumb into my temple to stop the thrumming in my mind. I didn't get headaches. Must have been the stress of the last few days. *Did I eat? When was the last time I slept?*

A touch on my arm pulled me from my thoughts. I snatched her wrist and held it firmly.

Lena narrowed her eyes. "You stopped walking."

I released her wrist and scanned the street around us once more. "This place—"

She took my arm and pulled me down the road. It unsettled me to see the glow from beneath the surface. I wasn't sure it was even safe to hold my weight because I couldn't quite see the pavement, but Lena didn't hesitate as she kept walking along. "Keep moving."

Her fingers were tucked in the crook of my elbow, and it took way too long for me to remember I was supposed to be making her suffer.

"What is this place?" I shook her hand off me and widened the distance between us on the street.

Daphne glanced over her shoulder but made no comment. She led us around the corner, and the street opened up into a wide open square. On the opposite end of the space, a Greek-style temple with stone columns rose up into the fog.

*Where were the police guys?*

I looked around, but there was no one. Not even in the shadows.

Daphne led us past a large statue in the center of the open square. The statue held my attention more than the other figures we passed in the city. A man held a woman in a lover's embrace while the waves crashed around them. There was something different about this statue.

"Who's that?"

Lena glanced up at the statue and then back at me. "Poseidon."

"And the woman?"

Lena glanced over her shoulder. Her face was filled with…reverence? No. Fear? "Kleito."

"Who's that?"

"She is the woman whom Poseidon loved. He built an island to be near her. Most of us are descended from Poseidon through Kleito." Lena kept her head turned to the street below us and avoided my gaze.

So, the people here were descended from the gods?

Daphne motioned for us to continue to the marble stairs. I scanned the statue again. What was Poseidon and this…Kle-woman doing in the middle of Atlantis? I mean, Poseidon was the god of the sea or something like that. But I had never heard of the woman.

Lena slipped back to my side as we climbed the steps.

"Be silent, Seth. I know you will want to say things to the council, but you don't know our ways. Please, just don't say anything. Especially not about the ring or your mother."

I grinned. She knew better than to give me a direct challenge. Ha! I would do the exact opposite. "'Kay, *Hel*-lena."

Her eyes grew wide. "I'm serious, Seth. They will—"

"Helena." Daphne motioned us into a room.

Lena put her hand on my arm and squeezed before walking through the open doorway.

I moved to follow her when Daphne blocked the way.

"If my daughter has cautioned you for some reason, perhaps you should take her warning."

The older woman's eyes were the same as her daughter's—full of mystery and secrets.

"Maybe that's what she wants me to do. And if that's what she wants from me, I'll do the opposite."

A slight smile on the woman's face made my gut clench. Did she want me to reveal who I was?

Well, good thing I didn't even know who I was at this point.

"May Themis bless you." Daphne turned and entered the room.

I thought I was prepared for what I would see on the other side of that door. I was wrong.

I entered as I had every other room since my military training—clearing every wall and corner in my vision. The interior was open, and the ceiling was stupidly high. A marble table extended several feet from side to side, like a conference table, but there was no seating.

Men and women entered from different entrances along the walls. Some were already present and stood around the room in clusters, discussing various matters and whispering to each other. Some glanced in my direction. Others ignored me.

Lena stood next to *him*.

The man with the smug expression and fancy hair. The man wore a similar toga, of all things. What a ridiculous sight.

When he put his arm around her waist, my jaw tightened. How dare he?

She was not mine.

But she certainly wasn't his.

I took a step toward her, and Lena's eyes locked with mine. What was that look in her face? I didn't know it.

She was never like this back home.

Daphne stood at the head of the table and folded her hands before beginning. "Gentle, gracious councilmen and councilwomen. I have come tonight with an unusual encounter."

Murmurs spilled into the room and sent a shiver down my spine.

"For centuries, we have been isolated behind the fog, unable to join the humans in their world and unable to reach the gods on Olympus." Daphne's eyes locked with mine. "A punishment for our sins so long ago."

"What sins?"

The crowd's whispers grew louder at my question, but I didn't care. "What sins?" I asked again.

"The sins of trying to achieve what the gods could not…" She walked to the corner of the table and lit her hand with the strange flame. "Perfection."

I chuckled, and her brow raised. I ignored the movement at the edge of my line of sight. The council was curious, not dangerous.

I motioned for her to continue. "Keep going. This should be good."

My eyes darted over to Lena for a moment. Enough to know that her face was twisted in a combination of rage and embarrassment.

My smile widened.

*Good.*

Daphne moved back to the head of the table and rested her hands on its top, delicately leaning forward.

"And we have paid a dear price for this isolation. Many of our own have sacrificed themselves to keep our vision going, their names forgotten by all for the glory of the cause."

Forgotten?

The word grated against my soul.

Those that sacrificed for a cause should never be forgotten.

What the hell was this place?

Daphne straightened, and a grin grew on her face. "But it seems that the Fates have been smiling on us and we ourselves are not forgotten." She lifted her hand out to Lena who, after a moment, left the perfect man's side and took it. "My own daughter, Helena, has brought us a chance for us to reach the human world and perhaps even Olympus."

The council's voices raised, and each member turned to their neighbor making exclamations about if this could be true.

"You see"—Daphne wrapped her arm around Lena's shoulders. "My daughter has not only chosen to return to Atlantis, unlike her flawed counterparts…"

*Flawed?* What did that mean?

"She has brought us one that is favored by Aite. Perhaps even carries her blood."

All eyes were turned to me in that moment.

"This is quite the claim, Daphne." A man with graying hair took several steps toward her before leaning heavily on his staff. "What proof do you have? Or do you want to ensure that your daughter's status is elevated and not cast down?"

My body vibrated with the alertness of an impending attack. What did they mean about *cast down*?

Lena...

What world did you come from?

Her eyes locked with mine, and the vibration turned to a humming in my mind.

Lena turned to her mother and whispered something in her ear.

"The young man she has brought back has spent all of his time in the human world. He has no knowledge of our ways. My daughter suggests that we earn his trust before making demands of him, Calix."

The older man narrowed his eyes. "It could also be a chance for you to teach him what you wish him to know of this place."

Lena left her mother's embrace and approached the old man. "Calix, I will vouch for him. He is...someone of great importance."

Calix laughed. "The word of a flawed? Ha! That is no better than the word of a lesser."

The perfect man in the toga put himself between Lena and the old man. "She will not be a flawed for long, Calix. Hold your tongue. The wedding is only two weeks away." He took Lena's hand and pulled her to the side, addressing the entire council. "Can we put this matter to rest?"

"The man needs to be taught our ways," commented one of the councilwomen. "He might endanger us without the proper knowledge."

"Lilith is correct." The older man turned and met my gaze for the first time. "I will take this *stranger* and show him our ways."

# CHAPTER 11

# Seth

I watched Lena leave the council chambers with the perfect man.

Dimos, they called him.

What a douche canoe name.

"You. What is your name?"

The old man hobbled closer to me and he smelled like tattered papers in a book. I wrinkled my nose and shifted my weight.

"Seth."

The man eyed me up and down before slowly turning and walking to the door. "Come, Seth. They woke me from my bed. I will show you Atlantis tomorrow."

"Where are we going?"

The click of his staff against the road grated my nerves. *Click, slide. Click, slide.*

Like Death himself had come at a snail's pace to haunt me.

"What's *your* name, old man?"

He turned and smacked his staff on the space in front of my feet. "Calix Ariti. And if you are going to survive in this place, you had better start paying attention to the details."

He swayed, and I reached out to steady him, but he waved me off.

"I'm not in need of your help young man. I am in need of my bed. Come. My home is not far."

I followed him back through the courtyard with Poseidon and the Kle-woman. I had plenty of time to study them since Calix moved at the speed of a glacier. The dark fog above us made it harder to make out their faces, but they seemed to be in love. They seemed...peaceful.

The memories of Lena leaning over my father's desk at the sawmill and her making food in my kitchen and her sitting on the beach, staring out over the vast ocean flooded into me.

Lena being wrapped in my arms was what love was.

Why had I come here seeking revenge?

I loved her.

I did love her.

She could say that things between us weren't real, but I fell for her the very first time I saw her.

I shook the thoughts from my mind and let the rage and desire for revenge swallow the memories.

*Love is damage.* That's what she said, wasn't it?

"Can you move any slower? I don't think it's possible!"

Calix chuckled. "Impatient. I like you already, Seth. Good news for you is that we are already here."

I looked at the marble steps, and something was oddly familiar. Where had I seen them before?

"I will have you stay in the guest quarters of my home. I don't know if they have been spruced up."

"I don't need much. Doubt I will sleep regardless."

"Why's that, young man?"

How had the old man climbed the stars with no difficulty? "It is rare that I sleep well. And I do not know this place."

The door opened, and a young girl with her head bowed stood to the side. Calix passed by her and never spoke to her once. She had the same three bars across her forearm as the lady I met when I first came through the fog.

"Down this way, Seth."

I snapped my head up—my focus had been on the young girl. Calix waved me down the hall and tapped his staff on the wooden door. "This will be where you stay. And don't try to leave. I'll know. There's no way through the fog for you."

I pushed the door open. "So everyone keeps saying," I murmured.

The door snapped back into place behind me, and my hand went to my glock. The room was dimly lit with the strange golden glow that was everywhere else in this place. What was it?

I tried to find where the electricity was coming from, but the glow seemed to run along the edges of the ceilings and walls with a life of its own.

In the center of the room was a modest bed. I sat on the edge and considered what I knew about Atlantis. Lena was worried that I would upset the council. Why?

It was a bunch of intellectual idiots.

Pretty much the same as Washington back home.

But if it were anything like my home, then they could be dangerous in their own way. I was dangerous with a gun. They were dangerous with words and power.

I took the gun from my back and laid down on the bed, shoes on. There wasn't any chance I was going to be caught off guard. I knew better. I had the training.

A sharp pain to my chest startled me from the sleep I didn't know had found me.

Calix hovered over me with his white toga and wooden staff and chuckled. "Did you forget to turn your ears on, young man? I imagined you would be able to hear an old man and his staff entering your chambers."

I pulled myself out of bed and tucked the gun that had done nothing to protect me into the holster at my back.

"It must be this place. I'm not used to the noises here."

Calix began to shuffle through the door of the room. "A poor excuse. There is no noise here. Come. Let me show you my city."

"What about food?"

Calix grinned over his shoulder. "That, we can agree on. Let us go."

I paid extra attention to the old man as we made our way down the marble steps of his home. Each of his feet glowed with the strange light as he stepped.

"What is that?" I pointed to his feet.

"Ah. I see you are finally beginning to pay attention. That, young man, is orichalcum. It flows from the blood of the gods."

"So you're…part of the gods?"

Calix laughed. "No. We are not the gods. The gods bicker among themselves and fight for who is the mightiest, the most clever, and who has the most beauty. No, we are *descended* from the gods. Most of us from Poseidon and Kleito. We harness the power of the orichalcum and use it to benefit us all and return it to the city itself. It is how we are able to have some version of normalcy in this prison."

"You mean the fog?"

"Mhmm."

Calix tossed me a fruit from one of the vendor stands in the street. "Here. Food."

I eyed the green and gold pear before deciding that it appeared the same as the ones back home. It tasted exactly the same as well.

He ate as we walked through the golden-lit streets. The fog above us gave the appearance of sunlight without the blue sky as a backdrop.

"Where are we going?"

"You are very impatient. Is it not enough that you take in the sights of the mighty Atlantis? Do you not see its power? Its majesty? Its beauty?"

I glanced around at the stone buildings and golden streets before shrugging.

"It's just another place, old man. I want to know where we are going."

Calix grumbled something and tossed the fruit to the side of the road. "The council chambers again."

"Why?"

Calix shrugged. "Just another reason, I suppose."

Was he…making fun of me?

We turned into the courtyard of the acropolis, and it was filled with people—a completely different scene than the one I had seen the night before.

"What is this?"

"The lesser marketplace."

It wasn't a marketplace at all. It was...a slave trade.

People in gray togas, some in good condition, some in rags, were lined up along a wooden platform in front of the statue of Poseidon and the Kle-woman. The men in black shirts stood with their arms crossed over their chests at every corner and in front of the people in gray togas. A woman in a flowing yellow toga stood at the center of the platform with an inviting smile. She called out numbers and motioned to each of those in the crowd as they bid.

This was an auction...of *people*.

How did that still happen?

"They're slaves."

"No, they are human," Calix corrected me.

"I'm human."

Calix turned and faced me, leaning heavily on his staff. "Are you?"

Lena's warning flashed in my mind. What did she want me to do? Confirm or deny?

No answer. That was better than anything I could think of.

*Damn.* I hated that Lena's advice was right.

"And this happens every day?"

"No, don't be silly. This happens once a week."

My mouth parted, and I wanted to spew a list of retorts to that statement, but the flash of golden hair on the steps of the acropolis stopped me.

Lena.

And the *perfect* guy.

"Aren't we going to be late or something?" I mumbled at the old man before pushing past him and moving toward the council chambers.

I followed the crowd into the same room from the night before and found a place where I could watch Lena. She hovered close to the *perfect* guy but did not directly touch him.

Daphne went and stood at the head of the marble table again and clapped her hands together.

"Welcome, council members. I'm pleased to bring our first order of business today to a start: the betrothal ceremony of my very own daughter, Helena Florakis, to Dimos Papadopoulos."

...What?

# Chapter 12

# Lena

Wasn't it enough that I had agreed to marry a man I did not love?

Was it necessary for the man who held my heart to be present to witness it?

"Dimos, do...do we...?"

"What is it, love?"

I tried not to cringe at the pet name. He assumed that I came back because I loved him. I did *like* him. He was a good match. He seemed to care about the important matters of our world, at least. But I came back for my dad. And now, I had this giant mess of heartache and problems. There was no way around this part, though.

If I was going to free my dad, I needed to marry Dimos.

If I was going to be in a position to help Seth, I had to marry Dimos.

If I wanted to save myself, I had no choice.

I closed my eyes to ask the gods to help Seth but stopped myself.

*Aite, don't let them know he is here.*

"Nothing. It's nothing, Dimos." I smiled up at him and hoped that he would buy my little lie. I wrapped my arm around his to try to sell it.

My eyes locked with Seth's. He wasn't going to leave this alone. His face changed from hurt to rage so fast that I didn't get a chance to react. Seth stepped toward me, but Calix smacked his staff on the floor in front of him, barring his path.

If there was ever a moment that I wanted to read his mind, it was this one. What was he thinking? Did he really not know? Had he ever paid any attention to me?

If he had, he would know that I did not want this union to Dimos. He would know that my heart belonged to him. He would know that I only had his best interest at heart.

But he didn't.

How could the man that I loved so deeply fail to understand me when I needed him most.

I bit my tongue so the tears wouldn't spill down my face. Perhaps love was not meant for me.

Gods above, what kind of life had I signed up for? Perhaps I was cursed.

My mother's words brought me from my thoughts. "In two weeks time, we will witness the union of these two and write their names in the council logbook."

"And the status of your child will be elevated." Calix did not show any shame for the insult he gave me and my mother. "May the Fates be merciful and bless you both with long lives."

Dimos took my hand and kissed the back, as was the tradition of our people. I smiled and bowed my head to show my agreement. Applause sounded around the council chambers and echoed through the pieces of my broken heart.

I wanted to tell Seth why. I wanted to give him some comfort, but the time for that had passed.

It should have been before I ever left Florida. Maybe even when he held the gun to my chest in my home.

*Seth...why did you have to follow me through the fog?*

*This was never supposed to be your story.*

I turned and stepped into Dimos's side with all my focus on avoiding Seth's gaze.

Calix returned to the marble table and tapped on it with his staff. Orichalcum glowed from beneath the table and gave the appearance of a lit altar.

*No.*

Seth wouldn't understand.

*This can't happen now.*

"Bring the lesser who tried to leave."

The enforcers dragged the young man to the center of the council chambers. He struggled and fought as his dirty black hair fell across his forehead. I almost called out Iason's name as they pulled him past us but I held my tongue. How had he fallen from a flawed to a lesser?

When I had left, he was on his way to a good match. He was going to be working as an enforcer in our world. What went wrong?

Behind them, a bound lesser with her blonde hair falling over her downturned face, followed the enforcers holding her lead.

Oh no. Iason wasn't that foolish was he? To fall in love with a lesser and try to run with her?

There was hope if they got past the enforcers. The flawed didn't have enough orichalcum to keep them bound within the cursed fog, and the human lesser would have had none in her veins at all.

But they didn't make it. They were caught.

Iason chose to stay for his choosing time. Did he regret that now?

I scanned the room for hope. Someone…anyone who would change what I knew was coming.

My eyes locked with Seth's, and I mouthed "no" to him. The confusion on his face broke more pieces from my heart. He was about to see first-hand the depravity of my world.

"It is not her fault, council. Rhea is not to blame," Iason yelled as he resisted the enforcers.

"What are the charges?" My mother's lack of emotion always frightened me. My body shook. This was my peer. My fellow flawed.

"Attempting to leave Atlantis with a lesser."

"Please, councilwoman." The girl spoke so softly I leaned forward to hear her. "If there is no forgiveness for Iason, let our ends be the same."

My stomach clenched. She should not have said that.

The council was vindictive about the rules. The rules were how the perfection of our city was achieved. No one breaks them.

No one.

"Put her on the altarium." My mother nodded to the table before her.

Iason screamed and struggled against the enforcers with a violent effort. Tears streamed down the girl's face as she was placed standing on the table. She brushed her hair back from her face, and the marks of the lesser seemed to glow in the golden light of the orichalcum.

"Be at peace, Iason." Her voice shook and broke as the tears fell harder. "I shall see you in the Elysian Fields."

With one purpose, all of those on the council lifted their hands and let the orichalcum release from their bodies and to consume the girl while Iason groaned and wailed. The light from their hands burned bright until she faded into nothing.

A single tear was all I allowed myself.

She had been blessed. The altarium was a merciful death compared to the alternatives.

When nothing of the girl was left, the orichalcum stopped, and the council members dropped their arms back to their sides. The only sound left in the chambers was the sobs of Iason as he mourned the love of his life.

"Now, what punishment is fitting for you, flawed?" My mother continued to move to the next order of business as if a life had not just been taken without need.

"The altarium," a councilmember offered.

Calix stepped closer to the marble table. "No. He will follow his love to Elysian Fields, which is exactly what he wants. No. Send him to the helpers. Let him be forgotten."

Dread climbed through my chest and choked the air from the room.

I had heard rumors of the helpers and the forgotten. How they drained those unfortunate flawed of their orichalcum to power the city, condemned to an extended life of torment.

"He is flawed. Orichalcum flows in his veins, though hardly enough to amount to anything."

My mother scanned the faces of those in the room before nodding. "Take him to the helpers."

The enforcers pulled Iason to his feet. Before they could drag him away, he stood firm and looked directly at Calix. "You are so foolish. We won't always be forgotten."

My eyes locked with Seth's. I could see he wanted to intervene. His moral compass was slightly broken, but he would never agree to what had just happened.

With the slightest shake of my head, I warned him from trying to fix this. There was no saving Iason, just as there had been no saving Rhea the lesser.

Life didn't need to be like this. Life didn't need to revolve around the power of our blood and the rules laid out by those who were most closely related to the gods. There had to be a way to free us.

Perhaps there was no saving any of us.

But with everything inside me, I was going to try.

# Chapter 13

## Seth

"Who are the most powerful gods?"

I glared at Calix. "Does it matter? They aren't here."

"Just because they are not here does not change that they exist. It does not change that they control power in our world."

"The big guy upstairs, the big guy in the ocean, and the big guy downstairs." I ducked just in time to miss Calix's swing at my head with his staff.

"Zeus, Poseidon, and Hades. They are not to be trifled with. They are not to be taken lightly."

"What does any of this have to do with this place? It's cursed. Isolated. Forgotten."

Calix's eyes seemed to glow for a moment before returning to their normal black. He furrowed his brow and hobbled past me in the library. "We are not forgotten. Come with me."

I pushed my way up from the wooden chair and followed the old man. My mind spun with ways to get to Lena. What to say to her. What to do to change the path we were on, but nothing seemed very obvious.

Calix stopped in front of a long wall with a drape in front of it. He pulled on a rope to the side and the heavy gray drapes lifted to the ceiling, revealing a mural. The painting on the wall seemed to stretch out forever. *How large was this building exactly?*

"This." Calix tapped his staff against a spot on the wall. "This is what Atlantis used to be like. It was full of light. The gods and goddesses walked among us. We were happy and fruitful." Calix hobbled further down the wall. "Here. Here is where the gods cursed us for our ambition." The painting faded into thick dense fog, mimicking the one that I had passed through. "No one with orichalcum can leave."

"Hold on." I crossed my arms over my chest. "Orichalcum? Explain. You've said that before."

Calix held his hand out and a dancing fire of light hovered above his palm. "Orichalcum. The power of the gods."

"And you have it?"

Calix narrowed his eyes. "All those who have the blood of the gods have it."

*Yeah, yeah…these people thought my mother was a goddess.*

My eyes passed over the room to a young man in drab gray clothes. I lifted my chin and nodded toward him. "Who is he?"

"A lesser." Calix leaned against his staff. "Why do you ask?"

"He's human. How did he get here?"

A twinkle sparked in the old man's eye. "Ah! Now you are starting to ask the right questions. I suppose this particular one was born here."

Calix began to move toward the far end of the mural. I jogged a step or two to keep up. "Is there another way he could have become a slave?"

"Lesser. There are no slaves here. This is Atlantis."

"Same thing."

Calix looked at me over his shoulder. "He could have walked through the fog."

Walked..."Wait, like from my world?"

The old man laughed. "Yes. But it is all our world. We may be cursed but we are the same world."

"So the humans are either born here or wander here by unfortunate circumstances."

"That's right."

"So what is a flawed? That's what they called Lena."

Calix turned to face me. "Ah...this is one of the...complexities of our society."

I glanced at the mural which now showed a beam of golden light piercing the fog of Atlantis from the inside out. That wasn't part of the history.

Calix cleared his throat. "We are not to fornicate outside of wedlock. It is what keeps some order in our society and it separates us from the frivolous nature of the gods themselves. However, there are times when an Atlantean might...fall to their baser natures and procreate with a human. These children are the flawed of our society."

"Seems mighty backwards to me to call a child flawed."

"The flawed are given an opportunity. We recognize, as did the gods, that they did not choose this life. They have the time of their choosing to either join Atlantean society or to leave to the human world. The flawed do not have enough orichalcum to bind them behind the fog."

"Well at least they have a fair chance."

Calix's eyes grew darker. "There is little in Atlantis that is fair. Remember that." He turned and headed down one of the rows of books.

"Wait," I jogged to catch up to him again. "If Lena is flawed, then her father is human. What happens to the human parent?"

Calix faced me. "The unfortunate lessers who parent a child here in Atlantis are sent to Elysian Fields."

"You kill them?"

He nodded. "It is how best we can raise the flawed in our ways." Calix turned and headed down the rows of books. "No more questions. That is enough for today."

I looked between him and the mural, with my mind sorting all the bits of information I had learned so far.

*What kind of hell had I stumbled into?*

# Chapter 14

# Lena

"Where are you going so early, Helena?" Kassia's curls bounced as she sped to catch up to me on the street.

"I have some reading I want to do today. It's been too long since I have seen the library."

My friend wove her arm into mine. "I'm glad I ran into you. Evander told me what happened at your betrothal ceremony last week. I can't believe that Iason would choose a lesser. He should have known better."

"Shh, Kassia. We aren't to say his name. He is forgotten."

She put her hand over her lips for a moment before she leaned closer to me. "There's no need to be frightened, Helena. You're practically one of us now. It's only another week before you are married to Dimos."

"I'm not afraid of becoming a lesser."

Kassia's eyes grew round. "I don't know how you could not be. Do you want to spend the rest of your days serving the elite of our world? Do you want to have to drink the isychia and have your will stripped from you? Do you want to be sold? Beaten? Raped?"

I pulled Kassia by her elbow to an empty alley. "Kassia, please do not remind me what is on the line. I was raised here, just like you."

She studied my face. "You're thinking of something. What is it?"

I dropped her elbow and returned to walking in the street. She caught up to me and asked again. "What are you thinking about?"

"There is something that I learned in the human world, and I wanted to see what our library had to say about it. That's all. Don't fret, Kassia."

I kissed her cheek and jogged up the marble steps to the building filled with history and knowledge before she could ask any more questions. I pushed open the large wooden doors, revealing the rows and rows of books in a room lit with orichalcum along the floor and the ceiling.

*Okay, Dad, I know that you spend a lot of time here for your master. Where did you read the prophecy you told me about? The one about "there will be a light that unfolds in this darkness…"*

He said, "So say the gods."

Dad didn't know about the gods until he came here. He must have read that in the library…somewhere.

I scanned my memory and my education for which of the gods would be most likely to say something like this. After all, the library was organized by the gods themselves.

Apollo was the god of prophecy. He was also the god of light.

I shrugged to myself. Seemed like the best place to start.

I wandered down to the section of the library where Apollo's records started. There had to be fifteen cases of books for this one god. Beside the section for Apollo was the section for Aite. It only had three books on the shelf. Part of me was tempted to spend my time there looking for something that would help Seth, but I needed to find whatever it was my dad was talking about first.

Or did I?

I shifted my attention to the shelf containing Aite's books. Taking all three, I went to a table close by and laid them out before me. The first was a general record of the goddess herself. The second was a list of ways she had cursed humans with her mischief and ruin. The third book was blank. It had her name on the cover, but the interior pages were empty.

Why was it here?

Was it a play on her powers and ability to blind humans?

I closed the books and returned them to their section.

Maybe Apollo would have better information. But where to start?

I walked down the aisles and pulled down the books related to prophecy and piled them around me myself on the table. Where could it be?

Something about light. Something about darkness.

I raised my hands over my head and stretched. This was going to take far longer than I realized. Why did it feel so important?

Maybe I was looking for something that wasn't even there—hope that there was a chance this world would be destroyed and the lessers would be liberated.

That the flawed would be free from fear of servitude.

My eyes drifted as the hours passed and the words blurred together.

Dad stood on the beach Seth and I had visited often with his eyes out over the horizon. His face was different than I knew it from before. It was...peaceful.

"I never thought I would see this again." The whispered words were barely audible over the waves. Were they meant for me?

"It's beautiful though, isn't it?" I offered.

He turned and reached his hand out for mine with a smile.

I returned his smile. The sand dipped around my feet as I took his weathered hand. Dad pulled me to his side and kissed my temple. I soaked in the moment, never wanting it to end.

"This is the most wonderful gift, Helena." His deep voice cracked on my name. "I'm so thankful to share it with you."

I squeezed his waist, and my heart filled with joy. He was free. He was here.

There was only one thing that could make it more perfect—

"Lena!"

I turned, and in the golden rays of the setting sun, Seth walked down the beach toward us. I hesitated, but he smiled at me, the real kind. The kind that melted any hesitations from my mind.

My legs started moving as my mind caught up to my body's reaction. I took off running.

Running to my Seth.

The one who held my heart.

The one whose soul was so entwined with mine that it was hard to tell where mine ended and his began.

The one who was the center of every desire and dream I had ever wanted.

He caught me easily, and I wrapped my arms around his neck. His hand pressed into my back and erased any space that might have been between us. I kissed his cheek and his neck before finding his lips. He met my kiss with a fervor of his own.

Oh, how I had missed his kiss. The real way. The way he showed me he loved me.

There was no guessing.

Each kiss was a confession of his love.

"Seth…"

"Lena. My Lena."

He released me enough to let me slide down his body and pressed his forehead to mine. I put my hands on the side of his face to keep this moment and store it in the memories of my heart.

Somehow, I knew that I was forgiven.

Somehow, I knew that all the pieces had fallen into place.

Somehow…this was everything I had ever wanted.

"Lena…"

"Lena…"

"Lena!"

# Chapter 15

## Seth

"Can you move any slower, old man?"

Calix dragged his left foot as he walked through the square. "You should focus more on learning our ways than my pace, young man."

"That's impossible when you lack the basic ability to walk."

Faster than I was prepared for, Calix smacked his staff on my shin. I bit on my cheek to prevent the yell from leaving my throat. He wouldn't earn that. I reached down and rubbed the area, dulling the sting.

"If you're able to move that fast with the staff, can we pick up the pace?"

Calix leaned heavily on the wooden staff as he chuckled. "I like my pace."

I straightened and crossed my arms over my chest. "Just point me in the direction of the library. I'll find my own way."

"No."

"What do you mean 'no'?"

"Are you unintelligent as well as impulsive?"

I knew the old man was goading me into a reaction, but it didn't stop me. I kicked the staff out from under his weight.

The golden glow of the orichalcum was brighter than the sun, and a pulse sent me flying onto my back. The stone scraped against my skin, and I lifted my hands to cover my eyes.

As the light dulled, the old man stood fully erect in the center of the street. His eyes blazed with the golden light, and he reached for the staff. To my surprise, it flew from the ground and into his outstretched hand. He smacked the end into the stone of the street, and the golden aura disappeared entirely, leaving the old man leaning on it as if nothing had happened.

I rolled to the side and pulled my gun from the holster. Before any thought could take me, I fired a double tap at Calix's chest and a third shot at his head. The golden glow formed a barrier between my bullets and the old man, incinerating them before they reached my target.

"Do you have a death wish, young man?"

"I've seen death more times than you, old one! She hasn't taken me yet."

Calix raised a gray brow. "She? Who said that Death was a woman?"

I rose to my feet and put myself nose to nose with Calix.

"My buddies who died overseas. My father. Does it matter?"

The old man smiled, and I wanted to snap his neck for the false identity of weakness he portrayed. "Do you really want to find out more about your mother?"

"Alleged mother. My father told me a different story." I tossed the gun onto the street. It was as useless here as I was, apparently.

"Your mother has been called Death by many."

"Alleged mother."

Calix turned and began to hobble down the street, and I followed him with reluctant steps. Maybe I was out of luck now that I was trapped in this God-forsaken city. My training was useless. My need for vengeance on Lena was fading.

The only thing I could think about now was solving the mystery of my mother. Lena seemed convinced that she was one of the Greek goddesses. If that were true, did my father not know or did he lie on purpose?

And then my mind turned to another small horror. Drew.

He was planning to come, for me. And there was no way to tell him that if he came, he would be trapped along with me.

"Here." Calix pointed his staff up the marble steps to a stone building.

How did any of the Atlanteans distinguish one building from the other? Even though I had been here, it was the same as all the others around the city.

I muttered a 'thanks' as I climbed the steps and pushed the wooden door open. There had to be a librarian or somebody around here.

It took me several minutes of wandering around to realize there was no one else here. I couldn't even find the mural.

"Great, now I'm lost in a library in a forgotten city. What could go wrong?" I mumbled to myself.

When I turned the corner, I saw her blonde hair scattered across the table.

"Lena!"

She startled awake and sent books tumbling to the floor.

"Seth…"

She pushed her hair back into place away from her face and stood quickly. I stepped close enough to see tears forming in her eyes.

What did she have to cry about? She was about to marry the one she loved.

Right?

She gathered the books up and pressed them to her perfect breasts. Lena went to move past me when I touched her arm.

"Are you alright?"

Her eyes snapped from mine to the hand that touched her arm and back to my eyes.

"I...I'm fine."

"Liar."

She pulled her arm away from my touch and stormed to the bookshelf, returning them to their places with a fury, causing more to fall. I helped her to pick up the books, and she pushed my hands away.

"I'm only trying to help."

"Don't."

"Let me help, Lena."

She lifted her eyes for a brief second, but I grabbed her chin so she couldn't look away. "Let me help."

Lena nodded and moved her face out of my grasp, but her eyes had already betrayed her.

She still loved me.

The knowledge wrecked me. My heart broke for my vengeance on her even as the truth of her love fused the pieces back together.

What had I done, seeking retribution? For what?

"Lena..."

She turned and put her hand on my chest, then removed it like I had burned her fingertips. "Seth, I'm marrying Dimos."

A knife turned in my chest. That was the only explanation for the pain coursing inside me.

"You love me." I whispered the words but I needed to see her reaction.

Her eyes dropped to the floor, and I waited, but not for long. When I stepped toward her, she raised her hand to stop me.

She took in a shaky breath. "I...It does not change my fate. I will marry Dimos."

"You don't—"

"I do."

Silence enveloped the two of us as I tried to tell her with my eyes everything I should have told her the moment I saw her again in this cursed city.

"What are you even doing here, Seth?"

I didn't want to answer her. It would break the moment, and she would be lost to me again. When she tilted her head and raised her brow, I sighed and answered anyway.

"I was here to find out more about this goddess you think is my mother."

"Aite." Lena turned and walked to another row of books while I followed her. "We don't have much, but this is all we've got on her."

"It's still three books." I shrugged. "Might as well start there."

Lena passed the books to me. "It's only these two, really. The third book was blank."

"Blank? Why is there a blank book in a library?"

"I'm not sure. I hope you find what you are looking for." She turned to leave, but I couldn't let things end this way.

"Lena—"

"Seth, don't make this harder than it has to be."

The tears falling down her face locked the words in my throat. She turned and jogged toward the door, and I had to watch her as if compelled by a spell.

This wasn't going to be the end of us. I wouldn't let that happen.

But one problem at a time...

I set the three books on the table and pulled the ring from my pocket. The ring matched the cover on the book—a circle with a horizontal line in the center.

Well, that wasn't a good sign—the old man was telling the truth.

I opened the first book and found a genealogy for Aite. She had no children.

Did that mean that I wasn't her child? Or did it mean that this record was written before I was born?

When I got to the last page, I dropped the book on the table.

A drawing, but it was undeniable who Aite was to me.

I had seen her picture more than once in my childhood.

My mother.

I collapsed against the back of the chair and stared up at the ceiling.

My mother was Aite, a goddess.

What did that make me?

A demigod? A god?

I shoved the thought aside. Better to understand what I could about my mother first and then figure out what was going on with me after.

I pulled the second book out.

*Aite is the goddess of mischief and ruin. Banished from Olympus, she left and made her way among men. Some even call her Death and give her the symbol theta.*

The symbol beside the words was a circle with a horizontal line in the center.

Great. My mother was a Greek goddess but she was in charge of ruin.

No wonder I made decisions I didn't want to answer for and burned bridges for fun.

I scanned the stories, but none of them were favorable. *Seems mother dearest spread reckless chaos wherever she went.*

At least we had that in common.

I set the second book on top of the first and slid the final book in front of me, the one Lena said was blank.

Why was it blank? Maybe I would find something different.

I opened the cover, and my shoulders slumped when I found it was empty, just as she had said. I flipped through the pages, and each one was the same.

It didn't make any sense. A book shouldn't be empty. It was supposed to have words and be full of knowledge.

I left it open to the center and stared, hoping for it to show something.

Still nothing.

Standing up, I paced and looked at the book. Why wouldn't it tell me its secrets?

I didn't know why but I was certain there was something more in this book.

I flipped the pages over again and paced around the table some more. My fingers must have brushed against the ring because it rolled a few inches across the table.

*The ring.*

My lips turned up, and I snatched the ring off the table top and slid it on my finger.

Words burst forth on the page, lit with the same golden glow as the orichalcum. I turned back to the beginning, satisfaction filling my chest.

*Dear Seth, I had hoped you would never find your way here to Atlantis, but with your father living so close, I knew it was possible. However, you must leave this place now. It is cursed. I have left you with the tools you will need to escape. Know that there is no normal way to exit. You carry too much orichalcum in your blood to be able to go back through the fog. It keeps orichalcum in. You will have to destroy it if you want to leave. I will do what I can to help you. I have stolen for you all the pieces you will need. Remember, when you don't see a way, make one. Love, Mom*

The smile faded from my face. The only way out was to destroy? How? And why?

This was Lena's home. Did I really want to destroy that?

But…if Atlantis were gone, she could be mine again.

I flipped the page and read on.

*I stole this prophecy from Apollo. It seemed valuable. "A light that unfolds in this darkness, beginning what will have no end. The forgotten will find their retribution. The innocent will become the violence." Use it well.*

I scanned pages and pages of notes. My mother explained how to use the orichalcum in the city, but she cautioned me on using it with others around.

*I have hidden the Eye of Poseidon in the temple of Kleito. It will protect you from those who mean you harm. I am trying to locate the torch that Poseidon stole from Zeus, but as I am banished from*

*Olympus, it is not an easy task. Find the Eye of Poseidon and you will be indestructible.*

What did a god's eye have to do with any of this?

*Finally, my son, the only way to accomplish the destruction of Atlantis is to join with the council. Take my advice. The ruin is sweeter when the destruction is complete. Keep those close to you who you consider your enemies. And remember that the heart is ruin.*

She wasn't kidding. Love was the whole reason I had stepped into the fog in the first place.

"Alright, Mom, you think I should join the council?" I whispered to no one in particular. "Sounds like the perfect way to plan their ruin—from the very center."

# CHAPTER 16

## Seth

*Shit.*

Why the hell was this harder than it looked?

The old man made it look effortless.

I closed my eyes and imagined pulling the light up from the ground and into my palm. Shouldn't it be easier if I was a demigod? That meant I had more of the orichalcum in my system than the Atlanteans.

A dull glow formed in my palm and I laughed. "Ha! There it is."

I reached over with my other hand to touch the light but it faded away. Shit. Shit. Shit.

Guns didn't work here.

My only weapon other than my fists was this light thingy. I ran my hands over the close shaved sides of my head and locked my fingers at the base of my neck.

Mom had said to pull from the inside. She said that it lived inside and around me.

Lena's face flashed across my mind. She could probably help.

I pushed the thought aside and dropped my arms.

THere was no way I would go to her while I was weak. She needed someone strong and I didn't even know how to make the power in my blood work yet.

So that left me with one option–find the eye of Posiedon so I was protected.

No, indestructible was the word my mother used.

That's what I needed to be to take on the council. Something didn't set right with me and those slimy political types. They were all the same. It didn't matter what country or city or culture they were identical.

They only looked out for their own interests. They used people. They broke the rules they made themselves.

And for all those reasons and more, they were dangerous.

I left the books out on the table and left the library to find the temple of Kleito. The buildings all looked exactly the same with the cold marble stone and gray steps.

"Hey," I tapped one of the guys in black on the shoulder. The bulky enforcer dude crossed his arms over his chest and raised a brow at my words. "I'm looking for the temple of Kleito. Can you help me out?"

"Kleito's temple was torn down decades ago."

*Seriously? Guess the Eye was lost.* I shrugged and grinned when a new idea formed. "Okay, can you point me in the direction of Dimos?"

The guy in the black shirt pointed down the street to the left. "Councilman Dimos' home is that direction."

I slapped the guy on the shoulder. "Great! Thanks!"

Somehow the steps to his home were different from the other homes around it. Maybe it was because it's where I saw Lena here first in this goddamn city.

I climbed the steps to his door and pushed it open. "Dimos!"

The humans in gray scattered as the door slammed against the marble stone and the sound echoed in the foyer.

"Dimos!"

Through the foyer I could see him sitting on a couch in the room past the stairs to his upper levels. He looked up at me as I approached and closed the book in his hands.

"Is there a reason that you are storming into my home, Seth? It is not customary—"

"I want a seat on the council." I stopped when I was only a few feet from him.

"Ah." Dimos set the book on the couch and rose to his feet. "I am not able to do that." He held his hand up to stop my impending words. "It requires a vote by the council. I am not able to do that on my own." Dimos lowered his hand back to his side. "I'm not sure that's why you have come though. If you wanted a place on the council, you should have reached out to Daphne. She is the leader of the council, not I."

The need to ruin and destroy was stronger in me now that I knew what it was. It rose up at Douche Canoe's words.

"No. That's not why I'm here." His jaw clenched and I stepped closer forcing him to look up to meet my gaze. "She's mine."

"Helena is my betrothed."

I gripped his throat and threw him to the floor. My movements were sure and swift and took him off guard by the look of shock on his face. I bent and leaned closer to him as I whispered, "She will never be yours. She's *mine*. She will *always* be mine. She deserves to have a love that…consumes her."

Douche Canoe flinched when I rose. Good. Golden light flooded to his hand as his senses returned to him. "I wouldn't do that if I were you, Dimos." I turned my back on him and began to leave the room. "I have more orichalcum than you and you know it." He didn't need to know that I couldn't access it yet.

I heard the rustle behind me as he scrambled off the floor.

"The wedding is in two days, Seth. There's nothing you can do to stop it. Daphne moved the date herself."

I paused at the door and met his gaze so he would know that I heard him.

"We'll see about that."

# Chapter 17

# Lena

Tomorrow was the day. It came too fast. I was supposed to have more time.

Tomorrow I would marry Dimos and secure my place in our society as an elite. It took me the entirety of the last week to try to forget about my run-in with Seth at the library.

Shit, who was I kidding?

I had thought about him more than I should have. He didn't even love me anymore.

Not to mention, I had crossed too many lines to turn back now.

And the whole reason I came back was to save my father from this slavery. It wasn't right. I couldn't leave him behind now.

"Do you want blue or purple lilies?"

"Does it matter?"

Kassia looked up from the arrangements. "Helena Florakis, of course it matters. Dimos is an important member of the council. And you are a councilwoman's daughter."

I shrugged.

"What has gotten into you? Your wedding is tomorrow."

It had everything to do with the fact that my heart was not in this marriage, but I couldn't tell her that.

"Helena? Did you hear me?"

I moved to the window and stared down at the golden-lit streets. "I heard you Kassia. Dimos is a…wonderful match. I have just been distracted lately."

"Oh?" She dropped the flowers on the table and joined me near the window. "It wouldn't have anything to do with the man who came with you, would it?"

"Seth didn't come with me—"

"Didn't he?" Kassia closed the wooden shutters and tugged me over to the sitting area. "He arrived nearly the same day that you did. He knew you from the human world. Evander said the council believes he is a demigod."

"It's not true."

"I don't believe you, Helena. What are you hiding?"

I took Kassia's hands in mine. "My friend, please do not press me on this. I asked Seth not to follow me. I expected him to listen to me and I never imagined he would come here."

She smiled as the edges of her eyes glistened with unshed tears. "But you care for him?"

I placed my hands back in my lap and found an invisible string to play with on my white toga.

"Helena, you must have some attachment to this man."

My tears came without warning, and I buried my face in my hands. "Kassia, I beg you to leave this alone."

"But...who is he? And why has the council not forced him among the lessers?" I sobbed harder, and Kassia put her hand on my shoulder as she spoke. "It doesn't make sense. Why did he even come here?"

"I love him." I dropped my hands from my face. "For the love of the gods, Kassia, stop...talking...if only for a moment."

To my friend's credit, she ceased her endless musings on the subject. I let the tears fall while my heart broke some more. I didn't know it was possible. I thought I was broken enough.

Kassia handed me a bit of cloth, and I wiped away the tears. "You love him?"

"Please don't make me say it again," I whispered.

"But what about Dimos?"

I met her eyes. "I will marry him tomorrow."

"But you love another. That's so...well, it's tragic."

I took Kassia's hands in mine again while sucking in a steadying breath before releasing it with my anxiety.

"I will not be the first person in history to marry a man I do not love. I'm sure I will not be the last either."

"And what about Seth?"

I closed my eyes and saw his face, his smile, his eyes in my mind. "He will choose whatever suits him. He always has."

Kassia dropped my hands, and I opened my eyes back up to the present. She picked up the flowers again. "Alright, Helena. Blue or purple?"

I offered her the smallest smile. It was all I had in me, but her lead was welcomed.

"Blue."

My friend guided me through what seemed like a million tiny details of the wedding that probably should have been decided the moment I returned. I let numbness and hurt overtake me and sat with my broken heart.

The day was nearly over when Evander entered through the front door.

"Oh, Evander. We are almost done here." Kassia stood and crossed the room to greet her husband. I watched in resignation, knowing that tomorrow my duties as a wife would begin.

It would only be for a short time…just until I found a way to free my father and the other lessers.

But it would be for a time.

"Was your day alright, darling?" Kassia placed her hand on his cheek and smiled as she asked.

"It was a quite unusual day."

Kassia moved to the edge of the room where a lesser poured three glasses of wine, as was customary at the end of the day. Evander and Kassia hardly noticed the man as he handed them their glasses.

I couldn't look at anything else.

I didn't know his face, but I would remember it.

His fate was the same as my father's.

The same as mine could be. As it would be if I didn't marry Dimos.

I cleared my throat and stood. "I must be going. Thank you for your help, Kassia." The two of them walked with me to the door, and a thought dawned on me.

"Evander, what was unusual about this day?"

"Oh." He shared a brief look with Kassia before continuing. "We had a new member join the council."

"No one has joined the council in years…"

Kassia placed her hand on Evander's arm. "Who was it?"

We said his name at the same time.

"Seth."

He was the only one who could join. Did he tell them about his mother? Did he confirm it?

How foolish could he possibly be?

"I must be going. Thank you for the information, Evander, and the help, Kassia."

"Enjoy your last night, Helena. Tomorrow you will be a married woman and an elite."

I smiled at my friend, trying my best to convince her that I was ready. Or was it me myself I was trying to convince?

Down the steps and onto the orichalcum-lit streets, my feet carried me while my mind wandered.

If Seth made the wrong move on the council, they would send him to the helpers for his dissension. It didn't matter how much orichalcum flowed in his veins. There were enough enforcers to subdue him.

And if they knew how much orichalcum flowed through his veins…perhaps they would send him to the helpers anyway to break the fog.

I stopped on the steps of my home with my hand on the door.

Seth needed to be warned.

I had to see him.

My heart ached, but he had to know.

When I turned to go back to the street, I startled at the bronze-colored eyes that met mine.

"Dimos...what are you doing here?"

"Can't a man see his betrothed?"

I pressed my back against the wooden door. "Of course."

"Were you leaving or coming?"

Oh gods above, which was the right answer here?

"I just arrived."

He stepped closer so I could feel his breath on my cheek. "Are you going to invite me in?"

"N-no."

He raised his head. "No?"

"It would make the marriage contract void..."

Dimos stepped back, but not enough to make me any more comfortable. "There aren't many who adhere to that law. It was Kleito's law. Not Poseidon's."

"Even still...I can't take chances. You know this."

He placed his hands on either side of my face and pressed his lips to mine. I let him lead me through the kiss. I wished I didn't have to be here for this part. Would my heart always resist his kiss? Would I eventually forget Seth and let myself love Dimos?

When it was over, he kissed my cheeks and took my hands in his.

"I cannot wait for tomorrow to be here. You will be mine, and we will be the happiest of couples in Atlantis. Even Poseidon and Kleito would be jealous of our union."

I forced myself to reach up and kiss his lips to silence the lies he didn't know he was telling.

Dimos released me and walked down the steps. "I'll see you tomorrow, my bride."

"Tomorrow," I whispered as I slipped inside my home. I slid down the door and brought my knees to my chest. What was I thinking? Seth made his choices. I made mine. I whispered the words to remind myself of my mission. My goal.

"Tomorrow, I'll crush my heart again and set my eyes on freedom. Freedom for all the flawed."

# Chapter 18

# Seth

I felt the thrum in my veins as I flexed the orichalcum, bringing the light to my palm. It wasn't easy following Aite's advice. My mother had left clear instructions for accessing the strange power, but who the hell would have thought that there was literal *power* in my blood?

The glowing light held for several seconds before fading again.

*Damn.*

If I were the demigod of ruin, shouldn't this be easier?

I slipped my shirt over my head and went to the door of my room. Calix stood on the other side in his ridiculous toga, leaning his weight on his staff.

"You're up early, old man."

I pushed past him, and he hobbled along behind me. "I could say the same to you. What were you working on in there?"

"It's none of your business."

"If it's happening in my home, I have the right to know."

I glared at him over my shoulder as we exited his home and onto the street. "Fine. I'll tell you at the council meeting. Also, why do you insist that I keep coming with you? It's boring and pointless."

"Even those things that lack thrill have value. It is how our society stays together. It is how we rule."

"Ha! Your society is isolated. Stuck. No one even knows you are here." I turned my body to face him and looked him eye to eye. "And no one ever will. Your council has been trying to undo what the gods did centuries ago. What makes you think anything will change that now?"

His eyes narrowed, and his nostrils flared. I struck a nerve somewhere, and it took every ounce of the little restraint I had to keep from smiling.

"We are almost at a solution. You are new—an outsider. You will not learn. You will not listen. What could you possibly know about our ways? Of our struggles?"

I cocked my head and turned to swagger off down the road. "Oh, nothing. Are you coming, or do I need to carry you, Calix?"

The old man grumbled as he began walking behind me.

I allowed myself the grin now that my back was to him.

Another skill that I recognized I possessed since learning more about my mother—I knew every button a person had. If I wanted to get under their skin and force a reaction, it was as easy as speaking.

Dad spent many years of my childhood teaching me restraint and discipline with my words.

Did he know who my mother really was?

Either way, I credited him for what self-control I did possess.

"Why have you not done away with me like the other humans yet?"

Calix stabbed his staff into the ground and turned to me. "You are not like other humans. At least, that is what Daphne says. She says you are like us—with blood of the gods in your veins."

"And no one wanted to confirm that? You just let me walk around unsupervised?"

"Who says you are unsupervised?"

"You're an old man, Calix. Feeble and weak."

The slightest smile lit his face as if he held a great secret. "I am an old man. Let's leave it at that, shall we?" Calix turned and resumed his ridiculous stroll toward the acropolis where the council met.

I glanced at the square, and something seemed…strange about the way it was set up. Somehow, it was more sad than it had been before. There were more enforcers. More of those humans in gray.

"What is this all about?"

Calix waved his hand with irritation at the enforcers setting up a wooden platform in front of the statue of Poseidon. "It's for the trials of the lessers, but it is not set to happen until tomorrow."

"Trials?"

"Another part of our culture you can learn about *tomorrow*."

I took several moments to watch the humans. They kept their heads down and scurried into the alleys as the enforcers set up the platform. Were they afraid of it or of the enforcers? Or both?

"Keep up?" Calix called over his shoulder.

I jogged the last few lengths to the steps of the acropolis, wondering what tomorrow held.

"There's supposed to be a wedding tomorrow. Won't the trials interrupt the wedding?"

Calix didn't need to know that there was, in fact, not going to be a wedding, but that was for a different person's pretty ears.

"The trials will be before the wedding. Business before celebrations begin."

He continued up the steps, oblivious to my attention resting on the platform still. Specifically, the T-shaped post that stood in the center. It wasn't a hanging post. Was it for whipping?

It would have to wait. I would know tomorrow.

The council members still eyed me with caution as I entered the room. Did they have any idea who I was? They should be afraid of me. I was here to fuck them up.

"Calix. Seth. I am so glad the gods saw fit to let you gather with us," Daphne said gently as she extended her hand and gestured for us to join those gathered around the table.

No one sat down. Everyone stood around the same table where the woman was murdered.

Maybe I should call it an altar. That seemed more fitting than table.

"Don't mind us. The old man couldn't hobble fast enough. I offered to carry him, but he has too much pride." I looked anywhere but at Calix, even though it would have been so satisfying. He must be seething.

"I'm sure that Calix came at his own pace, Seth." Daphne raised her brow as if to chastise, but the subtleties of politics were lost on me. Especially now that I knew who I was.

I was chaos—ruin wrapped in muscle and skin, ready to strike.

I shrugged. "If you say so." I glanced around at the faces of the council members, each wearing their strange white togas. They were watching. I had their attention, so I leaned against the altar with my elbow. "I had something I wanted to bring up anyway since I'm finally here after dragging behind the old man." My eyes darted to Calix, and the tips of his ears might as well have been smoking from how red they were. "I want to claim a place on the council."

Murmurs of dissension rose up through the room.

"What?" I stood and hopped on top of the altar and walked around to each of them as I spoke. "I carry as much—no, more orichalcum than everyone in this room." I pointed my finger and turned in a slow circle. "You. Can't. Deny. Me." I pulled the ring from my pocket and held it between my thumb and forefinger, raising it high in the air. "I am the son of Aite, and I demand a seat on the council."

The whispers and disgruntled words were bolts of energy to my soul. I lapped them up like a dog desperate for water.

"Council. Council!" Daphne raised her voice for the first time since I had met her. It reminded me of Lena, and I almost smiled.

The voices settled down, and Daphne motioned with grace for me to stand beside her.

I jumped off the altar and landed next to her, meeting her gaze with a challenge of my own.

"Well?"

"You know nothing of our ways—"

"You can't deny me."

Calix hobbled closer. "Does he even know how to access the orichalcum? His claim is invalid without it."

I reached deep within myself and let the golden light flow in and around my body with more ease than ever before. Golden light skimmed the edges of my vision and, in my periphery, there were beings moving who weren't there before. Who were they?

"How's my claim looking now, old man?"

Calix grumbled and tapped his staff on the altar. "Enough showing off. His claim is valid. See that he is written in the records of the council."

"You do not have the authority to order that, Calix." Daphne positioned herself to face the elder councilman.

Calix waved his hand in dismissal. "It doesn't need a vote or your approval, Daphne. He's made his claim perfectly clear."

Daphne looked to the scribe along the wall and gave him a subtle nod.

"That's it?" I looked around the room. "No vote?"

"The orichalcum spoke for you. There is no denying your parentage. The power of the gods is within you."

"Cool."

I began walking toward the door when Daphne called out after me. "Seth. You have responsibilities here. You can't just be part of the council. You will have duties!"

I waved my hand in the air. "Tomorrow. I'll deal with them tomorrow."

There was somewhere else I needed to be.

Someone who needed to know where I stood in life.

*My* Lena.

# CHAPTER 19

# Lena

The lights had dimmed in Atlantis for the night hours, and I lay in bed, staring at the ceiling of my home.

I should have been sleeping.

If not sleeping, then I should have been planning a way to get my dad out of Atlantis.

Or Seth.

Neither one should be here.

No human should be.

Seth being here could destroy all of Atlantis if the gods got wind of what I knew the council was working on—breaking out of the cursed fog. The gods would descend and destroy us forever if they knew we were attempting to break the curse.

The silence stretched out into eternity.

No wind. No night creatures. No stars.

The human world was full of noise.

Atlantis only had the strange hum of orichalcum.

And silence.

*Plunk!*

I sat up straight in my bed and swung my legs over the side. The sound broke the monotony of my insomnia.

*Plunk!*

This time, I noticed the sound coming from my window, which was covered by a wooden pane. What was it? There was no rain here. No birds. Nothing like in Florida.

I pushed open the panes and gasped.

"Seth! What the hell are you doing?"

He tossed one of the small stones up in the air and caught it. "What does it look like?"

"Like you're throwing stones at my window."

He stuck his tongue out and climbed his way up the wall of my home and inside to my bedroom.

"Why did you need the stones when you could have just knocked?" I crossed my arms over my chest and backed away from him.

He dropped the stones on the floor and closed the wooden panes. "It's more romantic to throw stones at a girl's window."

"Seth…"

He closed the distance between us and settled his hands on my hips. I stared at his chest, unable to meet his gaze. I couldn't bear to think he might still love me just to look in his eyes and see hate resting there.

"Lena." He tucked my hair behind my ear and lifted my chin. "My Lena."

"No…don't do this, Seth. Don't say—"

"I love you."

My eyes snapped up to his. The smile reflected the man I fell for in Florida. "No…"

"I can't ignore this, Lena. I don't care what you did to me. I love you." He tugged me closer, and my traitorous hands snaked up his arms.

"I'm getting married."

"You don't have to." He guided me back until my legs hit the bed behind me.

"I do."

"You don't." He pushed me gently on the bed. "You don't have to marry him."

Seth took his shirt and pulled it over his head, showing every inch of skin trapping solid muscles beneath. My breath caught because I had forgotten what it was like to be in his presence. Images of us from our past rushed in and reminded me why I couldn't think straight around him.

"Seth…"

He pulled my night clothes up to my thighs and knelt between my legs. When he kissed my inner thigh, I wanted to push him away as much as I wanted to pull him closer.

"Lena…tell me what I want to hear." His breath tickled my skin.

"N–no."

He grinned, and every stone I set up around my heart to protect myself turned to dust. "Perhaps I will have to ruin you first."

Seth climbed up the bed, and I put my hand on his chest to keep him from placing his lips to mine. Once that happened, I would be more lost than the city I lived in.

"You wanted to kill me. Remember?" I reminded him.

"A fit of passion. That's all."

"You held a gun to my chest."

"I would never kill you, Lena. You know that." He pressed closer, the inches between us dwindling away.

"I stole from you."

His lips brushed against mine as he spoke. "You stole my heart long before you stole my ring. No more talking, Lena."

I let my hand fall away, and his lips crashed into mine. Tears fell down the sides of my temples, and I gripped his face between my hands as if he would vanish in an instant.

Was this moment real? Was it a figment of my imagination designed to protect my heart from breaking further?

My legs wrapped around his waist, and he cupped my breast, forcing a moan from my throat.

"I've missed this..." He whispered the words as his lips trailed down my neck.

He rose up above me, and the look on his face was wild and untamed. He gripped my night clothes and ripped them open, spreading them away from my body. Seth kicked off his shoes and dropped his pants, leaving his entire and perfect body on display in the subtle night-glow of the orichalcum.

"Seth, come here." I reached my arms out for him, and he wrapped me up tight, crushing me to him.

"Tell me, Lena."

He wanted to hear me say that I loved him too.

He wanted to know that I felt the same as I did before I left him in Florida.

I did. I really did.

But I was getting married tomorrow, and it would be more cruel to tell him that I loved him and marry another.

So instead, I pulled his face to mine and kissed him. I poured every feeling and emotion into that kiss.

His cock twitched against my abdomen, and I reached between us to stroke him.

*Don't ask me for the words, Seth. They will ruin us both.*

Seth hovered for a moment before he took control and thrust himself deep inside me. I moaned and arched my back while his fingers dug into my hips.

Our eyes locked, and I couldn't decide if it was more merciful to cross the river Styx or live in this moment. Seth was everything I could have had in the human world. He was everything I wanted here, but it was not meant to be.

He moved inside me as his tongue trailed my collarbone, lighting a fire in my veins. My legs locked around his thighs, and I held him as close as our bodies would allow.

His rhythm turned into a frenzy, and I dug my nails into his back to keep from screaming out his name.

The warmth built in my core before exploding through every nerve in my body. No one had ever come close to making me feel like Seth did.

Tears fell in tiny rivers down my face, and I begged my heart not to break in front of him.

A moment later, he paused as his cock twitched inside me, and as he came back down to reality, his eyes locked with mine.

"Lena?" The sadness in his voice broke me.

"Just hold me, Seth."

"Did I hurt you?" He hovered over me with concern marking his perfect face.

I turned on my side with my back to him. "No. You didn't hurt me."

Several moments of silence dragged on before he finally slid into the space beside me and wrapped his arms around my waist, drawing me close. "I don't want to hurt you, Lena."

"You're not hurting me. It was everything I missed and needed."

His arms tightened around me. "Lena, you don't have to worry about anything. I will fix this. I promise. I love you."

I squeezed my eyes closed and flexed my fingers on his forearm so he would not say anything more. He couldn't know about my dad or setting the lessers free.

If he knew, he would help me.

And if he helped me, he would be sent to the helpers.

And if he was sent to the helpers…

Well, I would never see him again.

# Chapter 20

# Lena

The golden glow of the orichalcum peeked in through the edges of my window panes. Seth's arm laid heavily on my stomach, and I listened to his breathing, slow and steady. I turned my head to study his face.

One last time.

Once I married Dimos, Seth would never forgive me.

The tension in his forehead had melted away. His mouth parted slightly, and there was peace covering his face—the face of the demigod of ruin.

I did that. I brought him peace.

Was I making the right choice?

I swallowed and reminded myself of the lessers. Of my dad.

Dimos had almost as much power with the council as my mother did. With his resources, I would be able to free so many from the slavery they were condemned to.

At least, until he found me out…

But that was a problem for another day.

Step one…marry Dimos.

Step two…break my heart.

Break *his* heart.

What would Seth do when he realized what I had done?

It would be a mistake to marry Dimos. But my biggest mistake was coming back to Atlantis to begin with.

I slid Seth's arm off my naked stomach and put my pillow in my place. He didn't move or wake.

And I almost wished that he had.

That he had woken up and begged me not to marry Dimos. Convinced me that life would be better for us, for everyone, if I just…stayed.

But he didn't. And I was glad.

It was only a dream—one where I got everything I wanted.

I dressed quickly and took one last look around the room, delaying the inevitable. When I finally worked up the courage, I memorized every little detail of Seth while he slept, while he was peaceful, before I forced myself out my door.

I bit my lip and held back the tears. It wasn't fair. It didn't have to be this way.

Maybe I could go back?

Maybe I could tell Seth?

*No.*

If I told Seth about trying to free the lessers, he would help me. He would destroy the fog and Atlantis and release the wrath of the gods for breaking the curse not only on us, but on the human world too.

One foot in front of the other, I pushed myself to pull away from Seth. It was protecting him. This way, if anything did go wrong, he wasn't involved.

"There's the lovely bride!" Kassia called from the steps of her home.

I gave her a smile, and her face turned to concern. She picked up the fabric of her toga and came to me, putting her hands on my cheeks.

"What is it, Helena?"

"I...I am betraying my heart, and yet, it must be done." My throat constricted, and all that followed was a sob.

Kassia pulled me into her shoulder and wrapped her arms around me. "Helena, it must be done."

Her soft words cut through the confusion in my mind, and I gathered my breath. I let her guide me up the steps. She was right. There was no other path.

"Lesser, fetch me cold water," Kassia ordered a young girl.

She led me to the seating area from the day before and she dried my tears. "You can't be crying when your mother arrives."

"Will she be here soon?" I lifted my face and hoped that I had enough time to pull myself together.

"I am here, Helena." My mother stepped into the room. "What is the meaning of this?"

I stumbled up to my feet. Of course she would find me here—crying on my wedding day that she had personally arranged.

My mouth opened to speak, but no words came out. There was nothing I could say that would explain this.

"Speak, Helena! You are not made of marble. Why are you crying?"

I glanced at Kassia and back to my mother.

"I...I d-do not love him."

It was the only thing I could say that was true and would make any sort of sense in her world.

My mother scoffed. "This has to do with the demigod, doesn't it?"

I bit down on my cheek. There was no response that would be worth the punishment.

She marched to me and gripped my chin in her fingers. "Love has nothing to do with this, Helena. Forget love. Forget the demigod. Love will only ruin you here, daughter."

Only one tear escaped. I managed a curt nod while my lip trembled.

My mother dropped her hand but held my gaze. "You have so much potential, daughter. Do not destroy it now."

She gave Kassia a nod, and with the help of the lessers, they began to ready me for my wedding. They twisted my hair with flowers and dressed me in a white gown. Kassia pressed red rouge to my lips, and I forced my mind to separate from what was about to happen to me, quietly resigning to my fate.

A commotion at the front of the house drew my attention. Raised voices continued until they came closer and closer. I jumped to my feet, wondering what was happening.

A group of enforcers pushed their way past the lessers trying to redirect them away from the seating area. The hair on my arms raised, and my back stiffened. What were they doing here?

"Helena Florakis?"

"What is the meaning of this?" My mother rose and put herself between the enforcers and me.

"We are here to collect her, councilwoman."

"Collect her for what, exactly? She has a wedding in only a few hours."

The enforcer turned his black eyes on me. "The flawed has been accused. She is required to appear at the trials of the lessers."

"No…" I whispered.

"There has been some mistake, enforcer. This is my daughter, and she has a wedding."

The enforcer handed my mother a rolled up piece of paper. She took it and opened it slowly. Her eyes scanned the words, and then she shoved it back to the enforcer.

"Where is the accuser? I want to see them for myself."

The enforcers moved around my mother, and two of them took my arms, forcing me to go with them.

I was too stunned to move. Too shocked to resist.

Not that it would have mattered.

"Mother?"

"Helena, we will get to the bottom of this."

"What did it say?" The fingers of the enforcers would absolutely leave marks on my arm. I grimaced as they tightened their grips when we went down the steps.

"It says that you are accused of breaking Kleito's laws."

My head was underwater for all I could hear after that. My mother continued to harass the enforcers dragging me to the trials of the lessers.

I had broken Kleito's law.

I had slept with Seth before I was wed.

And he was not my betrothed.

But who would know that?

Or was that even the law that was broken? Kleito had many laws, but most of them were no longer enforced.

We turned the corner in the street, and the wooden platform was already set. The accused lessers were lined up and tied to iron hoops in the stone wall of the alley beside the agora.

My flight response finally awakened at the sight of what awaited me, and I kicked and pulled on my arms, trying to get away.

"No. There's been a mistake. Stop! There's been a mistake!"

The enforcers only dragged me closer and closer to the platform that would be my doom. How did this happen?

I saw Dimos crossing the agora in his best clothes, all ready to go.

"Dimos! Help! Something happened."

He paused when he saw me tangled in the middle of the enforcers before jogging up to us.

"Dimos. Help me."

He looked me over. His eyes were gentle, and he reached out his hand to push the hair from my face.

"Sweet Helena. Who do you think put you here?"

Dimos dropped his palm from my face and straightened as he nodded to the enforcers.

"Wait! Dimos!" The enforcers dragged me to the alley and chained my hands to one of the iron loops. "Dimos!"

I watched as he disappeared to join the rest of the council as the trials began.

I pulled on the chains and screamed to the sky. This could not be my fate.

I came back to help people. I didn't deserve this.

I wanted to pray—to ask the gods to help me.

My breathing came in quick pants as the thought settled in my mind.

It wasn't any use to pray.

The gods couldn't hear us here.

No one could.

# Chapter 21

## Seth

*Shit.*

*Where did she go?*

I threw back the covers and grabbed my clothes.

"Lena?"

The word echoed off the stone walls.

She wouldn't do this to me. Not again.

Would she?

Fuck...she would...

"Lena..." Her name fell from my lips as my heart dropped into my stomach.

There was still time—time to ruin her wedding.

I dressed and tried to pull orichalcum to my hands. The golden ray hovered only a moment before shimmering out of existence.

Shit. It would be really helpful right now.

I left Lena's home and ignored the way my gut twisted at her betrayal. Her *second* betrayal. She wouldn't get away from me without an explanation. A small smirk lifted on my face as I imagined the appalled faces of the Atlanteans as I stomped my way through the wedding ceremony, demanding answers from the bride.

The smirk fell, and a bitter taste formed on my tongue as my mind saw the douche canoe's face. Something wasn't right about that guy—like he had a permanent iron rod up his ass.

My shoulder bumped into someone, and I grabbed the man's arm. "Hey! Watch it."

The gray robes and the lines on his forearm marked him as a slave. His dark eyes locked onto mine instead of turning to the ground as so many of them did. There was something familiar about him.

"A light in the darkness…"

I dropped the man's arm and wondered from the gray streaks in his hair if he had lived here his whole life or had the unfortunate happening of stumbling through the fog.

"What?"

"A light in the darkness!" The man grabbed my shoulders and pulled me close. I almost knocked him to the ground, but there was something desperate in his eyes that stopped me. "The darkness finds your kind here. Beware the darkness or you will be forgotten."

I shook him away. "What are you talking about?"

"There is one…a light in the darkness…" The older man's eyes became cloudy, as if he were gazing far into the distance. He stepped back, and his eyes dropped to the street before he continued walking in the direction he was originally headed.

*What the hell…*

Raised voices pulled my attention from the weirdest conversation I'd had since coming here. In the square, a woman demanded to be heard.

The closer I walked, the easier it was to see the woman was Daphne. I didn't recognize her voice, and her expression was somewhere between fear and violence.

"Gather the council! I demand to hear from the accuser!"

Calix leaned against his staff. "The council will be here when the trials start."

"No! Before. I want to see them before the trials! There has been a mistake." Daphne squeezed her tight fists to her chest as she yelled.

"You know the law better than any of us, Daphne. She is a flawed and she has been accused."

"And you know what happens to the flawed that are accused! It doesn't matter if they are innocent or not…" Daphne covered her face with her hands before tangling them through her hair. "This isn't happening."

Calix placed a hand on Daphne's shoulder, and I closed the distance between us. I needed to know where she was. "Where is Lena?"

Calix's eyes shot to mine. "There is nothing you can do, young man. She is lost to us."

"Like hell she is."

I scanned the square for the answer and started moving as soon as I saw the guards in black. Those guys were the ones who would have the answers. A group of them hovered near the entrance of an alley.

"Hey!" I called to get their attention.

Three of them looked up as I approached, but I didn't care anymore. The flash of blonde hair was all the confirmation I needed.

It was more reaction than thought. When the first guard guy stepped in my path, my fist connected with his jaw. The second one grabbed my arm, and I flipped him on his back. The third didn't bother trying to stop me.

Her eyes lifted with the commotion, and I had never seen pure terror mar that lovely face until that moment.

"Seth! Stop! Go away! You can't be here!"

"Why not? I'm here, aren't I?"

Her hands were chained to the fucking wall. I grabbed the iron links and pulled with all my strength, but the chains held.

"Seth, leave! Go!" Her voice cracked, and I pulled on the chain harder.

"This is insane, Lena!"

"I don't want you to get hurt! Go!"

I dropped the chains and wrapped my hand in her hair, pulling her face up to look at mine. "No! You don't get to choose for me anymore!"

Tears streamed down her cheeks and…

And…

And I didn't know how to fix it…

Lightning bolts hit my back, and I dropped her hair.

"No! Stop! He's leaving!" Lena's screams didn't sound right.

More stabbing fire hit my back, and my knees buckled, falling to the ground. My face smacked against the pavement, and I cursed Atlantis. On every deity I could think of, I promised to destroy this place.

Cold iron locked around my wrists before the guards pulled my body up and dragged me to the end of the alley where they attached my own chain to the stone wall.

My head spun with the sting from the orichalcum and the lack of escape before me.

I looked for Lena, but she was out of sight.

This wasn't how it was supposed to go. Why was she chained to the wall?

A bell chimed in the square, and all the gathered crowd was silenced. Was this the start of the wedding or the trials?

Douche Canoe Dimos walked to the center of the wooden platform, and I wanted to vomit from the mere sight of him.

"We have several trials before the council today and we need your witness." He waved his hand out to the crowd as if he were inviting them to a fucking feast and not an execution.

That's what this would turn into.

Off to the side of the platform, Calix leaned against his staff, and Daphne leaned against him.

Douche Canoe motioned to one of the guards, and the trials began. The enforcer led Lena from the alley to the steps of the platform. A second enforcer approached her from behind, and Daphne moved between them.

"No. Not like this."

"Stand aside, councilwoman," the enforcer warned.

Daphne turned to Dimos. "This is your betrothed. Show her some dignity."

"She is a flawed, Daphne. A choice you made, not me. She will stand trial as every other flawed." Dimos motioned to the enforcer to carry on.

The enforcer grabbed the fabric of her toga-dress-thing and ripped it piece by piece until it fell to her feet and she stood naked in the square.

I couldn't stand the tears or the way her body shook as they pulled her to the center of the platform, completely bare and on display.

The damn orichalcum had stunned me so much, I couldn't escape the chains—but I also couldn't scream or taunt or even speak.

"Helena Florakis, you stand accused of breaking Kleito's law."

"How has she broken the law, Dimos? Be specific. The council will need all the evidence before passing judgment." Daphne went up the steps and joined Lena and Dimos on the platform. "It would be a shame if you didn't have sufficient evidence and accused a flawed unjustly. What would Themis say?"

"Of course, councilwoman Florakis. I have my evidence." Dimos turned behind him and motioned for someone from the crowd. A young woman was pulled to the platform by her arm. She glanced around the stage and out to the crowd.

"Kassia, share with the council what you know about the accused." I wanted to wipe off the smug look on Douche Canoe's face off with my fist.

"Um..."

"Kassia? Do you need some encouragement—"

"No!" The young woman's eyes widened. "No. Helena broke Kleito's law of purity for Atlanteans until they are joined with their partner."

"And how do you know this?"

"Sh–she told me."

Daphne grabbed Lena's arm. "That's not proof. She could be lying."

Dimos raised a brow at the young woman. "Is that all?"

The young woman's eyes locked with mine. "No. I saw the man enter her home last night."

"Thank you, Kassia, for your witness. You may go."

The woman ran from the platform, disappearing into the crowd.

Dimos walked in front of Lena and addressed the crowd. "This trial is simple. There is nothing to discuss. The flawed has broken our laws. She must be punished."

"It is an outdated law. One that we should rectify immediately." Daphne joined Dimos at the front of the platform.

"Even if we changed the law, it was still the law when the act was done. It does not change the judgment."

"The law was broken, councilwoman. A vote must be taken."

Daphne lifted her hand, and orichalcum flowed through her with a grace and ease I envied. The powerful light sliced through the chains holding Lena.

"My child has not committed a crime. She does not deserve whatever vindictive ending you are trying to create, Dimos. Do not punish her for our differences on the council."

Voices lifted in the crowd.

"Do not resort to violence, Daphne. That is beneath you."

Daphne invaded the douche canoe's space, and I had more respect for the councilwoman in that moment than any of our previous encounters. "This is beneath you, Dimos. A petty power grab. Using a woman's child against her? You should be ashamed."

"It was an opportunity, not a plan. That is all."

"Either way, it is an egregious accusation, and I will not tolerate this. We are a society that is above this type of behavior. The blood of the gods flows in our veins. Atlanteans have every access to knowledge and power and ingenuity, but you would resort to humiliation of one of our own—"

"She is not one of us! She is flawed!"

Daphne's entire body flared to life with the golden light. It hovered around her like a shield, and her eyes blazed bright. "Orichalcum flows in her. The blood of the gods flows in her just as it does you!"

"Diluted blood."

The light from Daphne's light struck out at Dimos, and he countered with his own orichalcum. The council and the enforcers joined Dimos. The collective group forced their orichalcum on Daphne while Lena screamed for them to stop.

The light grew in intensity, and I squinted, trying to see inside the flame.

Daphne arched her back and raised her arms, releasing more light until her form shimmered and vanished completely.

The light from the councilmembers faded, leaving an empty space on the platform.

Empty.

Gone.

Lena wailed and held her hands out to the empty space.

"I need your vote." Dimos nodded to the council.

"Guilty."

"Guilty."

"Guilty."

One by one, each member condemned Lena, naked and crying on her knees where her mother once stood.

The sight was etched in my mind, an eternal reminder of the pain and grief.

"Take her away."

The enforcers lifted Lena to her feet and took her back into the alleyway, out of my sight.

Dimos followed them down the steps and walked up to where I leaned against the stone wall.

"Now…what to do with you? The *supposed* demigod."

# Chapter 22

# Lena

*No.*

The word echoed around my mind.

None of this was real. It wasn't possible.

I wasn't accused.

I wasn't condemned to a life as a lesser.

I wasn't naked.

My mother wasn't dead…

The wind brushed across my bare skin, and the hairs on my arms lifted, reminding me it was true. All of it.

The enforcer didn't hold me quite as tightly now. He led me down the road, and I knew I was going to the helpers.

I didn't want the isychia.

That's not how this was going to end.

I…

I…

Kassia appeared in front of me. "Helena—"

"Don't."

"I didn't have a choice, Helena! He was going to charge Evander with a crime he didn't commit. He was going to send him to the helpers. Please! Helena–"

"Move!" The enforcer pushed my shoulder forward, and I stumbled.

"I don't care, Kassia. I hope the gods strike you down for this."

My friend's face fell, and tears streamed down her cheeks.

The ground beneath me seemed to tremble, and my veins lit from inside me. How was my body able to handle the heat of the orichalcum? This was more than I had touched before.

Kassia fled down the street, relieving me of her excuses.

I knew orichalcum. It lived inside me, but not the same way as with my mother.

This was different.

It was violent. And it frightened me.

*I* wasn't violent.

I wanted to help people.

On the edges of my vision, people moved as if a veil were pulled back and I could see another realm. The orichalcum seeped through my pores, and I closed my eyes as the light threatened to blind me.

I screamed and waited for it to end. The heat forced the tears from my eyes. This wasn't happening.

But my mother was dead.

And I was a naked flawed...no *lesser*...standing in the middle of the street. I clutched my chest and screamed for the stabbing in my heart to stop.

It was impossible to know anything but the swirling anger in my gut. I latched onto the emotion like a lifeline.

Anger smothered the agony and pain.

I rose to my feet and took my golden hand to the enforcer, laying it on his chest. He looked down at the orichalcum flowing around me and my hand.

His eyes met mine, and I pushed the orichalcum straight through his heart.

It was easy, with anger as my companion, to take the life of this Atlantean.

I pushed aside the old Lena who was kind and forgiving and gentle. She died with her mother.

New Lena had a mission.

I left the body lying in the streets. Someone would find it. Then my time would be up.

Maybe there was time for me to free him and escape.

My feet carried me all the way to Calix's home. I didn't slip down the alley like I had many times before. I marched to the wooden door and threw it back.

I moved through the servant's quarters until I found his.

"Helena, for the love of the gods, what is happening? Where are your clothes?"

My dad's brown eyes grew wide as the truth settled on him. He grabbed a gray toga from his room and handed it to me.

"We have to go."

"Your mind is still so clear. How?"

I took his hand. "Dad, we have to go. Do you remember the way through the fog?"

"They haven't given you the isychia yet," my father murmured to himself.

"Dad!" I took his shoulders and gripped them hard. "We. Have. To. Go."

His eyes refocused on me. "The darkness. There is no way through."

"You said there was a light."

"We can't leave without a light."

I pulled the orichalcum to my palm, and it flickered. How was I able to pull so much more earlier with the enforcer?

"Helena, there is no way out. They will find us."

I turned away from him. There had to be a solution. When I left, I was guided through the fog by a light, just like every other flawed before me. Maybe that would happen again.

"We have to try, Dad. That's the isychia talking. Listen to me. We have to go. Don't you remember what it is like on the other side of the fog? We can just walk through. All we have to do is make it there."

He sat in a chair, and his eyes unfocused. "It seems like it was all a dream."

"No. It's not a dream, Dad." I took the chair next to him. We had to get back there. "Do you remember the sun? The way it warms your skin? What about the human world? It's full of choices. Don't you remember?"

He closed his eyes and breathed out slowly. "Maybe…it's hazy."

"Dad, we have to go. Please. Now."

He opened his eyes, and there was a moment of hesitation before he nodded.

I took his hand and ignored the way the gray toga scratched and irritated my skin. The enforcers would be here soon. I ran as fast as my feet would carry me. Each step, Dad seemed more committed to escape.

Maybe there was a chance.

A twinge in my heart reminded me of Seth, but there was no way I would be able to get back to him in the center of the agora.

And I had to choose. I sent up a prayer to the gods to help him, even though I knew it was pointless. Those prayers bounced off a hazy fog above us, as useless as Sisyphus pushing the rock up the hill.

The stone and marble houses grew further apart, and the fog drifted closer to the ground. We were almost to the edge of Atlantis.

Almost there.

I never saw the orichalcum or the enforcers, but the pain of the light pushed me to the ground.

"Stop, lessers!"

We were too late.

I rolled to my back, and a hand gripped my throat, pinning me to the ground. The air in my lungs wasn't enough, and I pulled and scratched at the enforcer until he trapped my hands above my head.

"Don't move, lesser. You're both going to prison. And if I had to guess, you'll be headed straight for the helpers after that."

The enforcer's breath was hot on my cheek, but he let up on my throat. I coughed and dragged in as much air as I was able. His words sent ice through my veins.

No one came back from the helpers.

Once you got to the helpers…

Well…I'd be forgotten.

I glanced to my side, and an enforcer dragged my dad to his feet.

"Helena…what's happening?"

"Don't worry, Dad." I swallowed so my tears wouldn't fall down my face. He didn't remember what was going on. The isychia interrupted memory. Sometimes short-term and sometimes long-term. But either way, he and I were both headed to a dark ending, and he deserved some comfort. "Mom is going to fix this for us."

He nodded and followed the enforcer as we were led back into the city.

"Daphne…she said there was a light—a light that unfolds in this darkness, beginning what will have no end…"

He kept up his muttering as we walked. An enforcer gripped each of my arms with more pressure, and another one followed behind me.

Each step back to the city was heavier than the last. There was no escape.

At best, I would be given the isychia and live as a servant.

At worst, I would be sent to the helpers and be forgotten.

By the time we reached the prison, steady streams of tears were making their way down my face. I focused on the road before me to keep from falling down.

My spirit broke when they locked the iron chains around my wrists and led me into the white marble rooms of the prison. The enforcer slammed the metal door into place on his way out, and the silence screamed in my mind.

Begging for a solution.

Begging for a way out.

But there was none…

So much for a light in the darkness.

So much for the gods.

I was a lesser, and there was no way out.

# Chapter 23

# Seth

"Now…what to do with you? The *supposed* demigod."

Douche Canoe leaned closer to me.

His mistake.

I took my head and rammed it against his face.

Dimos reared back and howled as he clutched his nose. Blood was already streaming like a fucking river down his chin.

Good.

"Did you have something to say? Hmm?" I taunted him over his howls. "You said you needed to do something with me?"

A stream of orichalcum stabbed into my ribs, and I grit my teeth to keep the sound of a scream at bay. When Calix dropped his hand, I spit on the ground and tried to straighten my body, but the damn magic here was stronger than anything I knew from my old life. I sagged against the wall but did my best to get upright.

"That all you got, old man? Come on. Show me the good stuff."

Calix lifted his palm again, but Dimos put his hand on the old man's arm to stop him.

"Wait."

"Wait? He's clearly unstable. You can't possibly be thinking of anything other than the helpers for him."

Dimos narrowed his eyes on me. "He might still be useful. If he actually is a demigod, his orichalcum is stronger than any of ours. Combined with the orichalcum we have stored up, we might be able to break through the fog and reclaim our previous glory in the human world."

"Is that all you want? To get out of the fog? Great! That's my goal too." I gave him a half smirk. Maybe he would be foolish enough to—

"Free him." Dimos motioned to the enforcer, who moved at his order.

Calix straightened against his staff. "You can't be serious Dimos."

Dimos dabbed at his nose. "Why not? We both have the same goal. He could be…useful."

Calix smacked his staff down on the pavement of the street. "I want no part of this. I wanted no part of any of this." The old man turned and began to walk away from the square.

"You are still part of the council, Calix. You will be required to help us with finding a way through the fog."

"I'll be there, Dimos," he called over his shoulder. "Don't expect me to be cordial, though. I hope Zeus strikes you dead the moment we break through the fog."

Dimos leaned closer to me. "The old man is more useful to us alive than dead." He extended his hand. "What do you say we start fresh? As equals."

"Ha!" I crossed my arms over my chest. "By your own admission, I am greater than you." I leaned closer. "And even if we were equals, you would still be less because you use people. You deserve everything coming to you, and I hope I'm the one to bring it."

I didn't wait for him to answer. There was someone far more important than him.

"She's not with the others."

That had my attention. I turned and marched back up to the douche canoe. My hands smacked down on his shoulders, and I threw him up against the stone wall. "Where is she?"

"The prison. She killed an Atlantean and tried to escape with another lesser."

I dropped his body, and he sagged a bit as I and marched off in the direction of my Lena.

"You might want to stop calling her a lesser. She's more everything than you will ever be."

Dimos's voice called out to me as I left him behind. "Use my name and they will let you see her, but she has to stay there until her trial."

"Fuck that."

"If you are not able to abide by our rules, we will be forced to restrain you. Again."

I didn't answer Douche Canoe. There was no point.

Calix had pointed out the prison many times since I had been there, so there was no question where it was. I only wondered where exactly *she* was.

The inside of the prison was all made of white marble. There wasn't anyone when I first arrived, so I searched around and found a set of stairs. I hung close to the wall and kept my steps light. This was the strangest prison. Where were the guards?

When I reached the bottom, the room opened up into a wide space with no walls that seemed to stretch larger than this building itself.

People lay on stretchers, still and unmoving, as women in white togas with white hoods that clung tight to their faces walked between the rows.

My eyes kept darting from the unmoving people to the women.

Was it a hospital or a morgue?

I stared at one of the people on the stretchers and watched his chest. Why did he look familiar? His chest didn't move. It definitely wasn't moving.

A light tap on my arm set off my reflexes, and I held the wrist of one of the strange women with the white togas and hoods.

"Are you lost, Seth?"

"How do you know my name?"

"You are not forgotten."

My brows pinched. *What the hell?* "Uh…what does that even mean?"

She gestured behind her at the stretchers. "These are the forgotten."

"They look dead."

The woman shook her head. "Not dead. Forgotten."

I glanced back at the man.

The memory hit me. The guy, the flawed, who had begged them to kill him, but the council had sent him away.

To be forgotten.

A sick, swirling feeling moved around my stomach.

"So…are they dead?"

"No." The woman moved into my line of vision. "They are being harvested for their orichalcum. We keep them alive with as little as is necessary for life. The rest is being used for the benefit of us all."

"Oh, let me guess…you're a helper." The pieces of this sick world were starting to come together.

She smiled in a quiet way that made warning bells go off in my head. "I am. Helpers keep our society running in our own way. Why are you here, Seth?"

It unsettled me more the second time she said my name than the first. "I'm looking for the prison."

The woman raised her hand and pointed to the ceiling. "Those in prison are locked above."

"Right." I began to back up the stairs, looking at the greenhouse of almost dead people being harvested of their orichalcum. I clenched my jaw. No wonder my mother never wanted me around here.

Atlantis was a goddamn nightmare.

# Chapter 24

## Lena

How did I get here?

My body screamed as I started to lift my head off the cold marble floor. Tears streamed down my face as I remembered. My heavy limbs refused to cooperate, and my arm gave way. My elbow cracked against the stone, and I gave up—content to lie on the frigid floor.

Nothing was going right. My whole life fell apart in a matter of moments.

I should have stayed in Florida.

Or I should never have left Atlantis to begin with.

Why couldn't I start over again?

I would choose differently.

I would have said the words I wanted to say sooner.

It didn't matter. This was the end.

I pushed my hair out of my face and pulled the tattered gray lesser robes closer to me. The iron cuffs had already started to chafe my wrists.

Seth's face was all I could see, which surprised me.

My mother was dead, and my father was likely headed for the same fate.

But my heart wanted him. I wanted to know he was safe. I wanted to know they hadn't sent him to the helpers.

At least I knew that the gods hadn't found out he was here since we weren't destroyed. Maybe they didn't care.

Had enough time passed that the gods no longer remembered the curse? Or were we somehow hidden here? Did the fog also shield us from their sight? Perhaps they didn't even know Seth was here.

Or did they even know Seth *existed*?

The last one seemed most likely.

Zeus had banished Aite to the human world, forbidding her to return to Olympus. The god would be highly displeased to know that she had a child, but Seth's anonymity in our world would make it easier for her to hide his existence. Maybe Aite wanted to give Seth a chance.

Mother had told me over and over again about the dangers of trying to break through the fog. Atlantis might rise to its former glory, or the gods would be infuriated and destroy us all.

A commotion at the door pulled me from the grim thoughts, and I believed I was dreaming when the iron bars flew open.

Seth paused with his hand gripping the handle, looking like everything I ever wanted and everything I would never have.

"Lena…" His whispered words broke on my name.

I struggled to my knees, and he was there, wrapping me in his arms.

"Councilman Dimos said you can have ten minutes," the enforcer who followed him in ordered.

Seth squeezed his arms tighter around me. "Fuck that. I'll be here as long as I want."

"I'll be back when time is up."

The iron latch clicked into place, and Seth's lips were on mine. I cried harder, but he held my head in place, forcing me to feel everything I didn't want to.

Love.

Safety.

Hope.

Those were dangerous things to feel in Atlantis.

"Seth," I whispered to him.

"Lena, what the hell is this place? We're getting out of here."

I shook my head and buried it against his chest. "There's no way out, Seth."

"There is."

"I failed. I got him…but we didn't make it."

He pushed my shoulders away from him so he could see my face. "Lena, I can't leave. You know that."

I wrinkled my brow, and guilt hit me. "How did you find out?"

"It was in the books you found about my mother. Why didn't you tell me about the orichalcum?"

"You were never supposed to follow me here!" I covered my face. "I…I was the only one who should have come back. I was the only one who could leave."

He frowned, and anger flashed over his face. "And what? I was supposed to just sit by as the love of my life vanished into thin air? Fuck that."

"It was better that way…"

"Than what?"

"Than this! Seth," I raised my shackled wrists, "I'm a slave. And you will be forced to acknowledge me as a slave or be sent to the helpers. They don't just take the flawed…if you break the laws here, they will do it to you too."

"I'd like to see the council try to stop me."

"They already did, Seth! At the trial. And my mother was…she was the most powerful among us. She still died."

He pulled me into his chest, and I let him comfort me. His hand gripped my hair while his arm crushed me to him. "Lena, you know that I have more orichalcum than she did. I just need to learn how to use it."

I tightened my grip on his shirt, pressing myself as close as I could. His scent was burned into my memory, but I savored it here, waiting for the right words to come. "I can't bear the thought of you dying, Seth. Please don't do anything reckless," I whispered.

"Oh, like coming back to a backwards city with fucking crazy people in charge?"

A chuckle escaped my chest and surprised me. How was he able to find a way to make me laugh in a prison cell?

"Seriously, Seth…if the curse is broken and the fog lifted—"

The iron door slammed against the marble walls, and I jumped as Seth's arms tightened around me again.

"The lesser has a trial." The enforcers entered the small cell, crowding us. "Time to go."

"No—"

I cut Seth's words off with a kiss and hoped that it would be enough to keep him alive a little longer.

I poured everything into this moment, knowing there weren't going to be anymore moments like it.

No more feeling safe.

No more feeling loved.

No more more…hope.

It was our last moment together before everything would change.

Rough hands ripped me from Seth's arms.

"What the actual fuck? Don't touch her."

"Take it up with the council."

"Oh, I plan to."

Seth shoulder checked the enforcer as he passed them on his way out. He didn't look back. There was no final goodbye. That wasn't how Seth worked.

He was on a mission.

Whatever was going on in his mind, he wouldn't rest until it was accomplished.

"Let's go, lesser."

The enforcer's words scraped against my skin more than the iron shackles.

"It's back to the trials for you."

I hung my head knowing I wouldn't be alone at the trials. My father would be there.

Two trials in one day.

If I didn't know any better, I would think the Fates were involved in all of this. But Atlantis was cut off from all of the world, both human and supernatural.

I approached the agora, and it was infinitely worse than the first time. The first time, I was shocked. Now…now, I knew my fate.

I was a lesser.

As a lesser, I killed an Atlantean. I tried to escape.

I failed to escape.

I would be lucky to see Elysian Fields today, but I knew my path would lead to the helpers.

The enforcers pulled me to the wooden platform before all of our city. At least this time, I was clothed.

My father was brought up behind me.

I studied everything about his face. The lines around his dark eyes had deepened, and a heaviness weighed all around him.

At least when he died, he would go to the Elysian Fields in the underworld.

Mother was waiting on him…on us.

I took the smallest bit of comfort I could and latched onto it.

"The lessers have been accused of attempting to flee our city." Dimos climbed the steps to the platform as he spoke. "How do you find them, council?"

Before any vote could be cast, Seth swung himself up onto the platform. "What the hell is this?"

"It's a trial, Seth." Dimos folded his hands and eyed Seth with annoyance.

"You keep doing this and you won't have any people left to serve you. What are you going to do then?"

"Council?" Dimos ignored Seth.

"Guilty."

"Guilty."

"Your funeral," Seth said loud enough for all to hear.

The voices from the council died down.

"What do you mean, Seth? Please, speak your mind." Dimos turned his attention to Seth again.

"It won't take long for *someone* to start a rebellion and rise up against you. Keep suppressing people, and that's what happens. I've seen it all over the world. I'm surprised it hasn't happened here yet."

"Orichalcum is not present in humans, demigod. Something you would know if you knew anything about our world." Dimos turned back to the crowd of my people and addressed them. "Seth does make a point, however. I suggest we forgive the girl. She has not yet had the isychia and was distraught. That kind of ruling would be more popular with the lessers of our society."

What?

My mind began to race with reasons Dimos would allow this grace. What was he up to? In all my life, no one had ever forgiven a lesser for anything, much less a direct violation of our laws.

Seth's eyes darted from me back to Dimos. He dipped his chin, and Dimos nodded his head with grace.

"However, the man was already partaking the isychia. We cannot allow him to go without judgment."

My stomach clenched, and I whipped my head in my father's direction.

"Guilty."

The light from the council's orichalcum flashed, and he was gone in a moment.

No warning. No drawn-out moment.

Just gone.

"No!"

I fell to my knees.

He was standing there. He was…right there!

Then…he was gone.

I reached out my hand to the space where my father last stood. The world stopped moving, and everything around me fell silent.

My mission to free him was over.

Every decision I made since leaving Florida was for…

Nothing.

That's what I was.

Nothing.

A lesser.

…An orphan.

# Chapter 25

## Seth

I pulled her into my arms. Fuck Atlantis.

She didn't even turn her head into my chest.

"Lena."

Silent tears and a blank stare were the only answer I received.

"Lena!"

My chest wanted to cave in. I would do anything to protect her…

The orichalcum began to flow through me, but in erratic pulses, and no matter how much I tried, I couldn't hold it.

"Put her down, Seth." Calix somehow appeared at my side. "She has judgment awaiting her."

"Fuck that."

The douche canoe held up his hands to the enforcers who stepped closer. "There's a way we can help each other, demigod. Put her down, and we can talk."

I scoffed. "I'm not helping you." My arms tightened around Lena. Her body was shaking. Good. Maybe the shock was starting to wear off.

"You want to help the lesser—"

"Lena! What the fuck is wrong with you? She has a fucking name."

Dimos held his hand up to the enforcers again. "You want to help her. I want to free us from this curse. If the fog were lifted, there would be no reason to subjugate the humans around us. There would be more than enough willing to come and learn our ways. All we need is enough orichalcum to pierce the fog, and we are very close to that end. So I propose an alliance. Help me to lift this curse and you and the le—girl can go wherever you choose."

I looked down at the hollow face of the woman I loved. I wished to give her my will, my life, anything I had to make this better. She couldn't stay like this.

"Let her go, Seth. I'll ensure she is protected." Calix reached out his hand and placed it on Lena's arm. "I won't let her suffer. She will be safe."

I scanned the crowd in the square below the platform. There was no way to escape. The sheer number of people to get past would make the task impossible.

Resigned, I let Lena slip from my arms, and Calix guided her off the platform into the hands of the enforcers.

She wouldn't be like this forever. I wouldn't allow it.

Everything inside me was going to make sure she left this place. She deserved so much better than this world had given her.

"You all should be ashamed of yourselves for what you have become." I walked down the wooden steps of the platform and into the crowd where the councilmembers stood. "You had every chance to build a better society and you chose wrong. Creating slaves of humans, much less anyone, shows just how backwards and behind the times you actually are. The stories of the Atlantis of old, at least the ones in the human world, showcase your ingenuity and make you seem like the best place a person can live."

I turned in a circle and pointed at them one by one. "Each and every one of you deserves death and destruction for your choices. I hope I'm here to see it myself."

"That's enough, Seth." Dimos joined me in the square. A pale light hovered around him. Was he threatening me?

"It wasn't nearly the beginning of what you deserve to hear." I pointed to the statue in the middle of the square. "Kleito was human! And Poseidon loved her. Did you forget the ancestors of your society?"

The crowd stilled, and I wondered if they were frozen in place. How had I even remembered the woman's name? I rolled my eyes and began marching through the crowd that parted before me.

"Fuck this place! I hope the gods destroy you."

It didn't matter if they did or not.

If the gods didn't burn this place to the ground...

I would.

# Chapter 26

## Lena

My cheek was numb against the cold marble.

The enforcers had brought me food more than once. That meant it had been days since my parents died.

Why was I still locked in this marble cell and not marked as a lesser? I'd never known how it happened. Once a flawed was condemned or a human wandered into Atlantis, I assumed that everything happened at once.

I ran my hand over my forearm and pondered how much it would hurt to be marked.

Where was Seth?

What was he doing?

The door swung open, and an enforcer dropped more food on the floor next to the rest of my meals. "Eat."

I turned my body away from him. Death, even in the form of starvation, was preferable to the life ahead of me.

"She won't eat anything, councilman."

I lifted my head to see who he was talking to. Bronze-colored eyes met mine.

Dimos opened his mouth to say something, but stopped. His eyes searched my face, and I managed a scowl. He didn't deserve any words I could give him, so I turned back to the marble wall—the cold stone providing more comfort than any person in the room.

"We don't have a choice. Give her the isychia. I won't have her starve to death. She is the only bargaining tool we have with the demigod. He is…reckless."

What was Seth up to?

"Yes, councilman."

The steps of the enforcer echoed around my small room, but I knew I wasn't alone.

"Helena, you must underst—"

"Understand?" I turned toward the man who had condemned me to this life. "I know you aren't going to ask me to understand your choice to ruin me. Go away, Dimos."

I glared, and he continued to stare. What did he expect? That I would run into his arms and kiss his face?

"I didn't want things to be this way Helena."

"No shit. Go away, Dimos."

The enforcers returned and lifted me to my feet, my muscles resisting every motion with feeble effort.

"Take her and mark her. Then give her the isychia."

I knew this fate was coming, but it was still impossible to face it.

The enforcers took me to the other side of the building and chained my wrists so that my arms were outstretched. One of them approached me and put three of his fingers on my forearm. The orichalcum flowed from him, burning deep crevices into my skin. I winced and then screamed as the pain deepened. I panted in those brief moments before he did the same to the other side, dragging the light across my arm and branding me.

It was done. I stared at the marks, deep and ugly across my skin.

They would never go away. No matter what the ending of my story was…they would always be there—a reminder that I was worth less than others.

The enforcer gripped my jaw and pried my mouth open while another poured the isychia down my throat. I gagged and sputtered, trying to force the liquid away, but it only seemed to make things worse.

The taste of the isychia was not unpleasant, but I didn't want my free will stripped from me.

It settled around my soul and crept in the crevices of my mind, numbing as it went. I welcomed the relief from my pain.

My body relaxed, and the enforcers unchained my wrists.

Calix came into the room, leaning heavily on his staff as he looked me up and down.

"I'll take her from here." The old man tapped his wooden staff on the ground. "Come, lesser."

The more the isychia pulsed through me, the easier it was to pick up my feet and follow him.

Nothing was wrong…

The weight lifted from my mind and as it swam in the freedom of the poison in my system.

He led me to his home, and I smiled. This place was nice. It seemed familiar.

We went down the alley, and he led me into the side door. Shutting it behind us, something changed on his face when he turned back to me.

"Helena, I can't leave you like this. Hold still."

He slammed his staff into my chest and forced me back against the wall. The pain knocked my breath away, and I stared at where he pinned me down.

Golden light flowed from him and down the staff. My chest warmed and then it became too hot. I grabbed the staff, locking my hands into place.

Heat surrounded this...fog around me and running inside me.

And it *hurt*.

"Stop...stop please."

"No, Helena. You have to feel it."

I gripped the staff harder and pushed back. "Make it stop!"

"I didn't cause this pain. You can't stay in the fog. You're part of the prophecy."

*What?*

What prophecy?

With a final push, the light forced away the fog, and every vile emotion came rushing back in.

Tears streamed down my cheeks, and I collapsed to the ground as Calix retreated his staff. My mind flooded with memories and emotions cast aside while the isychia was present. I breathed and focused while the pain settled around my soul once again.

"Wh-what prophecy, Calix?"

The older man reached down and pulled me to my feet. Resting a hand on my shoulder, he dipped his head to stare at me eye to eye as he spoke. "A light that unfolds in this darkness, beginning what will have no end. The forgotten will find their retribution. The innocent will become the violence. That day will come when there is love of ruin."

Light in the darkness…

Ruin…

"Seth?" I whispered.

Calix nodded. "And I'm guessing you love him?"

I twisted my face. What did it matter if I loved him? There was no way forward.

Calix straightened himself and dropped his hand. "You do not need to acknowledge it to me. But Seth is indeed ruin. And love is what brought him here."

I covered my mouth with my hands and leaned against the wall. "You think he will break through the fog?"

"I know he will."

# Chapter 27

## Seth

"I know he will."

"What will I do?"

Calix turned to me, but I didn't care. I went straight to Lena and wrapped her in my arms, kissing her forehead.

"You're going to break the curse of Atlantis."

I grinned. "Oh, that's definitely going to happen. I plan to fuck this place up. Just need to figure out why I can't access the orichalcum as well as I should be able to." I pulled Lena tighter to me. "After I get her out of here."

"What?!" Her squeak of concern was cute.

"You're leaving, Lena. I can't focus with you here."

She shook her head. "I already tried that."

I tilted her face to see mine. "Not with me. Let's go."

"Don't stop until you can't go any further, Seth." Calix moved from in front of the door, and I nodded to him as we left his home.

I stopped with her in the alley and cradled her face in my hands. "Lena, you have to go back through the fog. I...I'll come for you when I figure this all out."

She shook her head, but I kissed her before she could tell me 'no'. I felt her tears against my face and I wanted to do everything, give her everything she deserved, but that future was only possible if she was still alive.

I pulled back and looked into her eyes. "I love you, Lena. I always have. I'm sorry I didn't tell you sooner." I kissed her for a moment before taking her hand and turning out of the alley. "Now, run."

And we did. We ran through the streets of this cursed city. I held her hand and guided her along the alleys until the buildings thinned and the fog loomed in the distance.

It was right there. So close.

And then I was zapped from behind.

I pulled through the ground to access the orichalcum around me. It flickered and sputtered but wouldn't hold.

More spears of violent light pierced me, and I groaned. "Lena!"

I saw them tackle her and bind her hands. My soul began to ache at how many times I had failed her. Over and over again. I should have been the one to help her and keep her safe. And she had spent far too much time in a prison for me.

The enforcers somehow managed to bind me with ropes that appeared to be infused with the light from orichalcum. I struggled against them, but they held steady. *How were they able to do this?*

"Let her go!"

Once my wrists were bound, the guards shoved me to my feet, bringing me face to face with Douche Canoe Dimos. If only he were a step closer, I would make sure he suffered.

"Take him to the helpers."

"No!" Lena's voice broke as she begged. "Please...no!"

Dimos faced her, and I wanted to rip out his tongue. "And this one—"

Calix appeared out of thin air like a ghost. "I'll be taking my lesser back."

"She needs to go to trial."

"You already robbed me of one lesser. No trial for her. I own her." The old man smacked the shins of the enforcers holding Lena, and they backed away from her. "Come, girl."

I never wanted to hug the old man more. If I were a hugger, I might...have hugged him for this. I watched him disappear with her, knowing that he would try to keep her away from it all.

"To the helpers. Take him now. Maybe the orichalcum in his blood is what we need to break through the fog."

The magical ropes burned and stung, and something dripped down my head. Was that blood?

I kept pulling for the orichalcum around me and trying to find enough to grab onto. Why wasn't this working?

Aite told me how to pull it in from around me, so why was it impossible?

They dragged me down the steps of the prison to the wide open room with the women in white. I fought and resisted as they threw me on a stretcher.

The same woman with the white hood appeared above me. "Hold him steady. I'll use the isychia to paralyze him."

She poured a liquid down my throat while the enforcers gripped my head and jaw. It burned like fire, but it didn't take long for a thick fog to hover in my mind. The edges of my vision started to cloud.

That's when the pain started.

Someone was ripping something from me.

I wanted to writhe away. I wanted to scream.

I wanted to put a bullet between Douche Canoe's eyes.

My body relaxed against my will.

Lena...

My Lena...

They would hurt her.

They would make her pay.

And there was nothing I could do about it.

My mind echoed with my silent screams while my essence was stripped from me.

I always imagined I would end up in hell if there were such a place.

Turns out hell was among the forgotten of Atlantis.

# Chapter 28

# Lena

"No, no…we have to stop this."

Calix closed the door behind himself. "Helena, you need to be patient. We can't go straight to the helpers. That's what they will expect you to do."

"We can't leave him down there!"

He hobbled past me, seeming to be more tired than before. "Be patient, for the love of the gods, Helena. We have to think, and I need to rest."

I followed him to the main living area and helped him sit on the chair as he put his staff across his knees. "I can't let anything happen to Seth. He…he…I didn't even tell him I loved him."

"Fetch me a drink, Helena."

I squinted at the command. Was it a command? I was his lesser.

A single tear started down my cheek, and I pushed it aside. This wasn't how it was supposed to happen. None of it was.

I brought Calix his drink, and he took it from me. We sat in silence while he finished. When he handed me the glass, he leaned back in the chair and set his staff beside him. "Let me rest, Helena. Then we will find a way to help Seth. The council only wants him for the orichalcum. We can negotiate with them, I'm sure."

I watched as his eyes drifted shut.

He was wrong.

The council would not negotiate when they had everything they wanted from Seth.

Both his silence and his orichalcum.

They would drain him from his unnatural life into eternity.

But…but maybe I had enough orichalcum to force the isychia away? Or enough for him to fight through it?

The beginnings of a plan started to form in my mind. I changed from the tattered robes of a lesser into a white toga of an Atlantean and pressed my hair into place after wiping away the grime from my face.

If the other lessers in the home noticed, they didn't say anything.

I went back to make sure Calix was still asleep when I saw a pair of daggers with silver handles hanging on the wall. It wouldn't hurt to have some other form of weapon. I wasn't sure that my orichalcum would work on Seth and I might have to drag him from the helpers' grasp.

I tucked them into their sheaths and slid them into the folds of my toga.

This was the only chance I was going to get.

The middle of the night in Atlantis could have been considered magical. There were no stars, but I didn't mind.

They had crossed me enough as it was. The orichalcum barely glowed off the thick fog as I traced my way back to the prison.

I had never been to see the forgotten, but we all knew where they were.

At times we saw the helpers coming and going, like a bad omen looming over us—a glimpse of what could be our future as the flawed.

I knew where the helpers slipped into the side of the prison and I went there.

No enforcers were around…and no helpers.

So…did they leave the forgotten at night?

I had no idea, but the opportunity was welcomed. The door gave way with ease, and I followed the hallway to an open room the size of the entire prison.

My heart broke at all the people there lying on stretchers.

Atlanteans.

My people.

They were so…still. I put my hand on the chest of the one closest to me. There was breath, but only barely. Did they know what was happening to them?

I weaved my way through the forgotten until I found him.

Seth lay perfectly still on the stretcher, and I put my hands on his chest. His heart beat beneath his ribs at a rate that was so slow I almost missed it.

"Seth…wake up," I whispered.

I forced myself to swallow and look at his whole form. Tubes were attached to his body, draining the orichalcum into containers on the floor.

What in the actual fuck?

I pulled the tubes from his body, hoping that would wake him up, even though I knew it was the isychia keeping him in place.

"Please…please," I whispered to the gods, knowing that they wouldn't answer. But I couldn't help myself. "Please wake him up."

I pushed my orichalcum into him and tried to force the fog back. "Wake up, Seth."

Nothing.

I let new tears fall and found the part of myself that held the most orichalcum—that violent force I ignored for most of my life. "Wake! Up!"

The golden light flew from my hand and into his chest.

"Stop!"

I looked up, my concentration breaking. An enforcer stood across the room near a staircase, and my heart dropped. He began moving closer, and I tried to get the orichalcum to move deeper but it…it…it wouldn't work.

Time slowed down, and I saw the future flash before me.

Seth would be tied to the forgotten for eternity.

I would suffer the same fate.

The gods would continue to ignore Atlantis.

Atlantis would continue to be cursed.

The lessers and the flawed would continue to suffer.

And I refused to accept it.

I pulled the dagger from my toga and dropped the sheath on the floor.

Seth wouldn't want this life. Either his death would mean we could be together in the Elysian Fields, or it would bring Aite's wrath onto Atlantis.

Maybe both.

I raised the dagger over his chest.

This...this was the only way.

Against my very nature, I had become the violence—a traitor to my own identity. I looked down at Seth's face.

I was Icharus, and he was my sun.

Unlike Pandora, I knew what misery and ruin I released on us all.

*May the Fates see fit to bless me, though I expect that even they did not see this end.*

I dropped the dagger into his chest as the sobs choked me.

"I love you, Seth."

The second dagger was far easier to manage. It fit between my ribs like it was always meant to be, despite the pain. Warmth flowed out of my chest and around where my hands held the hilt. I didn't feel my body fall but I lost sight of Seth as the darkness closed in around me.

In a matter of moments, I stood before the river Styx.

I looked around.

"Seth?"

He should be here.

"Seth?"

I turned in a circle, scanning the faces of those leaving our world and entering the next.

Where was he?

He should be here...

# Chapter 29

## Seth

The pain increased and then it stopped.

That must be how I died.

The fog around my mind lifted, and when I opened my eyes, everything was completely white.

"Hello, Seth."

A woman in a white toga with gold olive leaves in her hair walked to me.

So Death was a woman? Huh. Guess my dad was right.

I swung my legs over the side of the stretcher and looked around. No people were there. It was nothing but white.

"Where are we?"

She studied my face and then smiled softly. "Outside the gate to Olympus."

"What the hell am I doing here?"

The woman moved closer and tilted her face as she looked me up and down. "I intercepted the prayers of a beautiful Atlantean so I could meet my son."

That got my attention. I looked at the woman again. She seemed somehow familiar but...much younger than the pictures my father had kept of my mother.

"How do I know it's you?"

She chuckled and held her hand out for me to see. On her finger was a ring that matched the one on my hand.

"I kept one and left one with the man I loved...and our child."

I raised my brow. "Why did you leave? Why are you here now?"

She turned and walked a few steps away. "I suppose those questions have the same answer. Too much ruin in one place is destructive."

A throat cleared. A man holding a cane with a skull on the handle was standing to the side, staring at my mother. "I know you aren't planning something like this without my help are you, Aite?"

"Uncle, I didn't know you would want any part of it." Aite went to the middle-aged man and kissed his cheek. "Though, I can see how you might have an interest."

The man lifted his chin. "Who is this? I don't know him, but I should."

"Now, Uncle, I have brought you many lives over the centuries. Grant me this one life to be spared."

The man tapped his cane on her side, and she stepped out of his way. He limped as he approached me, using the cane to steady himself.

"Drop the Uncle act, Aite." He stood in front of me, one of the few people able to look down on me because of my height. "My name is Hades. What might your name be?"

"Hades?" I glanced at my mother. "As in god of the underworld?"

He lifted his cane and gave a mocking bow. "The one and only." He placed the cane before himself and put one hand over the other on the skull handle. "Now, your name, boy?"

"Seth."

"Hmm…Aite!" Hades snapped his fingers, and my mother was pulled to his side without any effort. "You have been up to a bit of chaos, haven't you. Tut-tut-tut. Your father would be highly displeased that you procreated."

"What price, Hades? I don't feel like playing games." Aite rolled her eyes.

"What is the price of a soul?"

"Save your poetry for Persephone! She is the only one who appreciates it. What is the price of *his* soul?"

Hades smirked. "A life debt from the little demigod of ruin and misery should do the trick."

"He stays in this world. Not the afterlife, Hades. He deserves that much."

"Hmm, I accept!" He turned with a bit of flare and put his hand in the space between us. "What do you say, *Seth*? Would you like to stay here in this world? Choose carefully! It is one or the other. I won't allow you to travel between them."

I crossed my arms over my chest. "What do you want me to do for you?"

"Whatever I want, whenever I want. I promise to not be…too unreasonable."

What the hell? Was I really about to make a deal with the god of the underworld?

At least if I stayed in this world, I had a chance of saving Lena and destroying Atlantis.

I put my hand in his. "Deal."

Orichalcum flowed out of the god's arm and locked a binding magic into me. A tiny dagger appeared on the skin of my hand, and all in a moment, Hades disappeared as if a ghost.

I looked around, but my mother and I appeared to be alone once more.

"He…he just does that? Comes and goes how he pleases?"

"Who knows the mind of a god? Hades is the most merciful of them all. Be thankful it was he who took an interest in you. My uncle has been kind to me, especially since my father banished me from my home."

"That sounds like a lot of family drama. I'll pass on that part."

"Well, son, we have our flaws, but just remember that I rescued you from your death."

"Thanks for that." I cracked my knuckles. "Now, how do we get back to Atlantis? I have some misery to handle and a douche canoe who has to die."

My mother smirked and she cut her eyes to me. "Would you like some help? Maybe I can teach you a thing or two about ruin and destruction."

"Yeah…that sounds like the kind of family reunion I can get behind."

"Let's do this."

Aite snapped her fingers, and in a moment, we were standing below the prison in Atlantis, surrounded by those forgotten.

I stood at the head of the stretcher where they had stolen my power. It took only a moment to see her blonde hair cascaded around her form like a waterfall on the floor, mixing with the pool of her blood.

"Lena?" I whispered, and my throat closed up because...she...it wasn't true.

I knelt beside her body and pulled her into my lap, the blood collecting more and more around us. There was a dagger between her ribs, and I pulled it from her body.

"Lena?"

My hands shook as I pushed back the golden hair from her face. Her eyes stared off into a distance I couldn't see, and I put my fingers to her neck.

I knew from the amount of blood on the floor that there was no way she could be alive but I had to be sure. I had to know if the woman I loved...if her heart still beat.

Nothing.

Not even a flicker of a pulse.

I had seen death enough to recognize it, but it marred my love's face and burned the image into my mind.

A deep trembling started in my soul.

It burned and twisted and screamed as it tore its way through my body.

The orichalcum blasted from me in a blinding light, knocking over every stretcher and shaking the very foundation of the building. Moans and cries rose up from the forgotten Atlanteans, but the orichalcum wasn't done. In my next breath, the light shot straight through the top of the building, through several stories of prisons, and clashed with the fog.

I felt the fog's presence and I felt the curse of the gods.

It didn't matter. The orichalcum channeled through me until I felt a pop and the fog vanished. The curse disappeared, and the Florida night sky shone down on me once more.

Sweat poured down my body, and I laid Lena on the marble floor. With her blood covering me, I rose and stood before the thousands of forgotten. *How many decades had they been collecting them?* Each of them looked at me, and my mother put her hand on my shoulder.

"Atlanteans. Your curse is broken. You are no longer forgotten."

I made a point to stare out into the crowd, infusing my words with the orichalcum inside of me.

"Now, go get your retribution."

# Chapter 30

# Seth

They didn't need any more prompting. They didn't even hesitate when the first of the enforcers arrived.

The forgotten Atlanteans destroyed them with a vengeance.

My body still shook with the rage of Lena's death looming in my mind.

"How about a little chaos?" Aite winked at me as she moved gracefully to the walls of the prison. She placed her hand on the marble, and lit it with orichalcum. I thought she was about to bring it crumbling to the ground when I heard the doors above us click open.

Prisoners fled their cells and poured into the street.

Something had shifted in the orichalcum since the curse was broken—it flowed easily.

Or maybe it was the range of emotions at the sight of Lena.

Either way, I knew I was unstoppable.

Atlanteans stepped into the streets and stared up at the night sky. I pushed past them. There was only one I wanted to see.

My mother danced as she walked, smiling and sending bits of orichalcum into the buildings like small bombs.

Her chaos was delicate and fine.

Mine was wrapped in fire and ready to destroy.

"Dimos!" I threw orichalcum into the council building as I entered the square. "Come out and face me!"

Atlanteans fled the square and into the streets around us.

I let loose my orichalcum into the statues of Poseidon and Kleito. The couple collapsed into the street before shattering into a thousand tiny pieces.

My mother approached the wreckage and lifted a small blue stone from the center of it, tucking it into her hand before crossing the distance to me.

"I didn't think this was here any more."

"What is it?"

"The Eye of Poseidon. I'm not sure how it got here. It was supposed to be in the temple. Trust me…you'll need it later."

I took the stone and put it in my pocket.

Before she could turn away, I grabbed her arm. "Mom, can you do something for me? When this is all over?"

She nodded, and I leaned in and whispered my request.

Aite pulled back to look at me. "Seth…are you sure?"

"I can't go to the underworld, but you can." It hurt to utter the words, but it gave me a small measure of peace. I turned away before she could question me further and began yelling in the square, "Dimos! Come out before I burn this place to the ground!"

Both my hands lit with orichalcum, and I raised them above me, ready to destroy everything.

"Wait!" Dimos appeared in the street. "Wait." He walked toward me with a smile on his face. "You did it! You actually broke the—"

I fired two rounds of orichalcum into his chest and another one between his eyes.

His body fell backwards into the street.

But it didn't bring her back.

It didn't give me any measure of satisfaction.

It didn't…fix anything.

"Seth?"

My mother called my name softly. And when I met her eyes, she blinked out of existence.

Did she know what I was doing?

I let it all come tumbling out. Orichalcum flowed from deep inside me. I pulled more orichalcum up from the streets and the earth.

The scream that left my chest didn't sound like me. It sounded wounded and broken instead of like the rage that thrummed in me.

She was gone.

She had no right.

She didn't have to leave me.

She…she really was gone.

The orichalcum pulled down every building here. Atlanteans fled away from the city and through the swamp that surrounded it.

My power wasn't satisfied until Atlantis was flat.

And when it was…the silence was welcomed.

I sat on a stone from the city and looked out over everything.

It felt good…and empty.

When the dawn started to peak over the horizon, I heard the flapping of wings. I smiled at the break in the silence and turned my gaze on to the sky.

I must have been losing my mind.

Was it a bird or an angel?

When the creature came closer, I recognized Drew's face. He flew above me with wings of white feathers. I should have been more surprised, but at this point…my friend flying above me like a fucking angel was the least of my worries. When he saw me, he dropped his wings close to his back and landed with a thump.

"You missed all the action," I told him as I stared back at the horizon.

"You could have waited."

"Eh," I shrugged. "More fun for me."

He looked around at the destruction of Atlantis. "And Lena?"

I rose to my feet and began walking back through the desolation and toward the horizon. "Dead."

"Seth…I'm so sorry."

"Don't."

I didn't look at him. If I did, I'd probably end up punching my friend in the face just for reminding me that my heart was not made of stone, but rather lay in shreds on the destroyed ground of Atlantis.

"Aite? Was she here?"

"Yeah…she was here." I pointed to his back. "I'm guessing you know her. What with the wings and all."

Drew shrugged. "I guess you could say that."

"Huh…"

Drew began walking next to me. We made it to the edge of the city before he spoke again. "I tried to come sooner. The curse wouldn't let me."

"Yeah...I know."

Drew bumped my shoulder. "What do we do next?"

I clutched the Eye of Poseidon in my fist and turned to give him a sly grin. "Well, there's a little issue with the god of the underworld, but until he catches up to me, how about we go and see what we can ruin?"

Drew grinned. "Lead the way."

# Chapter 31

## Lena

I sat on the grassy plains and wondered if he would ever come for me.

How long would Seth make me wait?

My heart yearned to be close to him.

I had crossed the river Styx and waited for him to come to the Elysian Fields.

My parents reminded me that this was happiness and this was peace.

But it wasn't for me.

It was endless waiting.

When would he come?

"Hello, Helena."

The soft feminine voice called to me from behind. I rose to my feet as I studied her face. I knew it from my education and the photos I found at Seth's home.

"Aite…how are you here?"

"I worked out a deal with my uncle."

"Where is Seth?"

Her face dropped a bit, but then her hand was on my temple, and I knew something was happening. Something I didn't want, but I couldn't stop it.

"I wish things were different, Helena. It was your prayer that I intercepted which led me to Atlantis. Seth made a deal to stay in the human world without knowing you had already died. He didn't want you to suffer, so he asked me to do something."

I began to panic because I felt the fog of the isychia start to cloud my mind.

"He wanted you to have peace. And the only way to do that here is if he didn't exist for you."

My heart pounded, and I clenched my hand around the goddess's arm but it was no use. "Please…don't…"

I felt the memories being pulled away as I clung to each and every one. Each one was part of my soul disappearing out of existence. I struggled to hold on to them.

The time we first met.

Our first kiss.

Our first time.

When he came to me in Atlantis.

When he told me he loved me.

But in the end, I was no match for a goddess. She stole them all from me.

Aite took my hand, and we rose together until we were facing each other. What was a goddess doing here in Elysian Fields? "Um…what are you doing here?"

She smiled. "Nothing, sweet one." She tucked my hair behind my ears. "I have one question for you and then I will let you get back to your parents. Do you know my son?"

I searched the recesses of my mind, but nothing would come. We had not learned anything in school of Aite having a son. Maybe I had just forgotten.

"Um…I'm so sorry, but no. I don't know who you're talking about."

She smiled and kissed my cheek.

"Don't worry, sweet one. All is as it should be."

The goddess blinked out of existence, and I breathed in the peace of Elysian.

Life was difficult and full of hardship before.

Now…my life was something wonderful.

# EPILOGUE

## Seth

I threw the dart and guided it with the orichalcum to the center of the board.

"That's cheating."

I glared at Drew. He was always a sore loser. "It's called using my resources."

"It's going to get us thrown out for sure."

I glanced over at the bartender, who was paying way too much attention to us.

"We're probably going to get thrown out no matter what we do."

Drew shrugged and lifted his beer to take a drink. "Wouldn't be any worse than the time Lena…"

He drifted off on purpose.

We didn't talk about her.

She was better off now.

Safe.

Loved.

Happy.

I knew the moment he was remembering. Lena and I had gotten so drunk last summer, she was dancing on the bar top with her shirt off and I was making an obnoxious amount of noise.

Well, I didn't remember it completely, but that's what Drew said.

He was always there to bail me out when things got bad, like it was his job.

Apparently it *was* his job…something my mother had put him up to.

Whatever. I didn't need him, but it was nice to have him around all the same.

The woman who had been eyeing us at the bar finally got the courage to make her move.

I wasn't sure why she was being shy. She had a body to die for and no problem with getting male attention. She pulled my darts from the board. "Care if I join you?"

Drew slammed his beer on the bar top and intercepted her.

"Oh, no. Love and ruin is a terrible combination. Move along."

The woman placed her hand on Drew's chest. "Do you have something to be afraid of, eudaemon?"

Alarm bells began to go off in my head. Who was this woman, and how did she know Drew?

"It took me a minute to recognize you. New hair? Different dress?" Drew lifted her hand off his chest and shoved it gently back in her direction. "But still the same old heartbreak."

"Aw." The woman patted Drew's cheek. "Let's leave the past in the past, shall we?"

She finally turned her eyes on to me and put her hand delicately between us. "Hello there. My name's Aphrodite. What's yours?"

I raised a brow and crossed my arms over my chest.

"I thought the gods were staying in Olympus."

She trailed her fingers over my crossed arms. "Oh…we were. But we sealed ourselves there at the same time we cursed Atlantis, and someone"—she tapped on my arm. "Someone broke that curse. I heard they dropped every stone to the ground."

I shrugged. "Wouldn't know."

"Hmm." Aphrodite grinned. "That's too bad." She walked around behind me and threw the dart directly to the center of the board. "You see…now that we are free to roam the earth again, I figured I would…come and start a new life."

She turned fast and came close enough to whisper in my ear. "What do you say we go into business together? I'm thinking love and ruin would be a great combination."

A grin came to my face.

Who didn't like a little ruin?

"I'm in."


The End

# Afterword

First of all...I'm sorry.

I know you all will be coming for my head after that one.

So I have good news and bad news.

The bad news is that Seth and Lena's story is complete. We may see the demigod of ruin again... only time will tell.

The good news is that this is not completely the end. Forgotten Retribution is a prequel to an urban fantasy series hopefully kicking off in 2025! Follow me on socials so you don't miss anything!

# OF DUSK AND DAWN SERIES

Of Dusk & DAWN

Delve into nine worlds of magic, fantasy, and romance with the Of Dusk And Dawn books, each written by a talented author who has created a story with a broken curse that contains the prophecy of Dusk and Dawn!

*Those Who Seek Vengeance* - **Christy Kenning**
| Secret Identity, Fairytale Retelling |

*Forgotten Retribution* - **Leigh Fields**
| Star-Crossed Lovers, Greek Mythology |

*Broken* - **Ada James**
| Forbidden Love, Secret Twins |

*Sacrifice for the Standing Stones* - **Bree Moore**
| Enemies to Lovers, Nature As Ally |

*Blade Upon the Vein* - **ASF DeWeese**
| Hidden Royalty, Enemies to Lovers |

*Web of Echoes* - **Courtney Davis**
| Tragic Past, Second Chance Romance |

*Sky Stitcher* - **A.C. Guess**
| Enemies to Lovers, Forced Proximity |

*Starlings in the Dark* - **Forest Moria**
| Gods and Mortals, He Falls First |

*Brightless* - **Teshelle Combs**
| Fated Mates, Light and Shadow Magic |

# ABOUT THE AUTHOR

An American fantasy and romance author, Leigh loves her family, a strong cup of coffee, and happily ever afters.

Mother to four wild boys and an ICU nurse on the side, she can usually be found in yoga pants or scrubs. (Aren't those the same things?)

When she isn't wrestling, refereeing, or loving on the boys, (or at the hospital) she can be found cuddled up with a fuzzy blanket, a bowl of popcorn, and a good book.

# ALSO BY LEIGH

### The Shadow Dragon Series
The Cord Between Us
The Pieces Around Us
The Stars Against Us
The Sword Above Us

### The Melody Chronicles
Mist Guild Archives

### The Twelfth Siren
A Cursed Covenant

### Legends of Cheia with Teshelle Combs
Sever and Split

### Tales of Ba'karan
Waking Flames

# connect with me

Want to keep up with the latest updates with my books?
Join my Facebook group Leigh's Dream Lounge.
Follow me on Facebook at Leigh Fields
Follow me on Instagram @authorleighfields
Follow me on TikTok @authorleighfields
Support me on Patreon at Leigh Fields